## "Lucca," she called softly to him. "Wake up. You're dreaming. Come on."

Using a gentle rolling motion, she managed to get him on his back. More unintelligible words flew out of his mouth.

His tear-washed face was her undoing. She bent over him and started kissing his eyelids and cheeks. "Lucca?" she whispered. "The war is over. You're home and safe." She ran her lips over every rugged line and angle of the face haunting *her* dreams. Her hands massaged his shoulders, willing him to relax and let go of the powerful flashback.

"Hush, now," she murmured against his lips, both of theirs salty from his tears. "You're not alone. I'm here."

Just when she thought she wasn't getting through to him he muttered, "Annabelle?"

"Yes!" she cried, so relieved he'd come back to reality she didn't care what he thought of her unorthodox methods. Her sorrow for what he'd suffered went too deep for tears. He'd been injured and had lost his best friend. She rocked him in her arms. With a swift strength she could scarcely credit, he pulled her body toward him.

**Dear Reader**

Up to the time I was fifteen, going on sixteen, our eight-member family got along with the Buick my father drove. (He looked exactly like Charles Boyer in his younger days.) Then something incredible happened. In 1955 he came home from work one day driving a convertible that was so adorable I thought I was seeing things. He'd bought a Porsche 356 Carrera Cabriolet. It was gleaming white, with red leather seats, and looked like a toy. I'd never heard of a Porsche, but if you could fall in love with a car, I did.

A month later it was time for me to take my driving test, and Daddy taught me how to drive in the Porsche with its stick shift. The day after I got my licence, he let me drive it to my high school. Needless to say I was the most popular girl at the school that day, and never got over my love of foreign sports cars. When you read this novel, HER ITALIAN SOLDIER, you'll see I still have a mad passion for them.

I dedicate this book to the most saintly, brilliant, wonderful, generous father in the world.

Enjoy!

*Rebecca Winters*

# HER
# ITALIAN SOLDIER

BY
REBECCA WINTERS

MILLS
BOON

First published in Great Britain 2011
by Mills & Boon, an imprint of Harlequin (UK) Limited,
Eton House, 18-24 Paradise Road, Richmond, Surrey TW9 1SR

© Rebecca Winters 2011

ISBN: 978 0 263 22101 5

Harlequin (UK) policy is to use papers that are natural, renewable and recyclable products and made from wood grown in sustainable forests. The logging and manufacturing process conform to the legal environmental regulations of the country of origin.

Printed and bound in Great Britain
by CPI Antony Rowe, Chippenham, Wiltshire

**Rebecca Winters**, whose family of four children has now swelled to include three beautiful grandchildren, lives in Salt Lake City, Utah, in the land of the Rocky Mountains. With canyons and high Alpine meadows full of wildflowers, she never runs out of places to explore. They, plus her favourite vacation spots in Europe, often end up as backgrounds for her Mills & Boon® Romance novels, because writing is her passion, along with her family and church.

Rebecca loves to hear from her readers. If you wish to e-mail her, please visit her website at: www.cleanromances.com

# CHAPTER ONE

ANNABELLE Marsh stood at the bathroom sink while she began removing her makeup. She didn't recognize the blond woman in the mirror staring back at her. There was an unnatural gleam to her shoulder-length hair she could never have achieved on her own. Her eyes really weren't that violet. Nor were her brows and lashes quite as dark.

Artificially flawless skin highlighted by a subtle bloom brought out her high cheekbones. The makeup artist had defined her mouth to make it look more voluptuous. Her fingernails and toenails possessed their own polished sheen.

She'd had a bevy of fairy godmothers doing what they did best as they'd transformed her. Marcella of Marcella's Italian haute couture salon in Rome chose all the designer clothes that Annabelle would wear throughout her photo shoots in Italy. She'd added jewels as the final touch for the shoot that had started four days ago at an air force base outside Rome in front of an MB-Viper fighter jet.

It had been a lark so far—loads of fun.

"Three weeks of being the Amalfi Girl," Guilio told her. "My wife and I will see to your every comfort.

Then—since you insist—you can go back to being Ms. Marsh."

"You mean the forgettable Ms. Marsh." She'd had long enough to stop grieving over a failed marriage and divorce two years earlier, and had taken back her maiden name. But a lack of self confidence, remained as one of its by-products.

His brown brows lifted. "If you were forgettable, I wouldn't have picked you for the most important proj- ect of my life."

Annabelle shook her head in disbelief. "I still don't know what you see in me."

"My brothers and I, the whole Cavezzali family, have been in the business of designing cars since World War Two. But I was the one who dreamed up the Amalfi sports car. It's been my life's work. I saw the lines of it in my sleep years ago and *lines,* Annabelle, are like the bones of a beautiful woman. What lies beneath de- termines what will eventually become a masterpiece."

She flashed him a teasing smile. "You saw my bones?"

"Right away. They spoke to me. They said, 'Guilio? At last you have found what you've been looking for.'" The charm and exuberance of the attractive sixtysome- thing Italian couldn't be denied. "I am going to form a marriage that will show a whole new face of the elegant world of the Italian sports car."

Annabelle would never forget that day two months ago when the dynamic car designer had come to the Amalfi dealership in Los Angeles, California. He and her boss, Mel Jardine, the owner of the complex who sold the most Amalfi cars in the States, had business to talk over. Guilio was launching a spectacular new sports car.

Being Mel's personal assistant, Annabelle had taken care of all the arrangements to make Guilio comfortable, including catering their meals. He'd insisted she remain for the day-long meetings and he was so attentive, she feared the married man might be interested in her in a nonprofessional way. But he soon dispelled that worry by bringing on another one. He told her in front of Mel he wanted Annabelle to be the model to advertise his new car.

She laughed at the absurd notion, but he kept right on talking while Mel shot her a glance that said she should listen to this Italian genius.

"I'm perfectly serious. For the last year I've been searching for the right woman. I had no exact face or figure in mind. I only knew one day she would come along and I would know her." He stared at her. "And here you are. You have that Amalfi Girl look. You're unique, just like the car. Mel will tell you I've never used a female model before."

Annabelle knew he spoke the truth. She was familiar with the brochures around the shop. They only featured prosperous Italian men in ads with his cars, like a businessman from Milan, or a socialite from Florence.

"I'm so flattered I don't know what to say, Mr. Cavezzali."

"Guilio. Please."

"Guilio, then. But why bring in a woman now?" She was filled with curiosity. "Out of the whole car industry, your ads are the most appealing just as they are," she assured him and meant it.

He tapped his fingertips together. "That's gratifying

to hear, but I want this campaign to be sensational. It's in honor of my brilliant boy." The hushed quality in his tone told Annabelle how very deeply he loved his son.

"Lucca went to military school at eighteen and has distinguished himself as a fighter pilot with many decorations to his credit." His eyes moistened. "He's my pride and joy. I've named my latest creation the Amalfi MB-Viper to let him know how much I admire what he has accomplished."

Ah… Now she understood. He'd named his new sports car after the fighter jet his son flew.

He gazed at her for a long time. "I want your picture to adorn the brochures, the media ads, the video and the calendar I'm having made up to commemorate the launch. Every Amalfi dealership around the world will be sent posters and calendars ahead of shipment to create excitement about a whole new market of future Amalfi sports-car owners. Be assured I'll have security with you at every shoot for your safety."

When Annabelle got over being speechless, she said, "I'd be *honored* to play a part in its launch."

Someone else, like her ex-husband Ryan, would be speechless, too, when he saw her picture on the calendar. He'd dreamed about owning a flashy sports car when he'd finished his medical residency. One look at the new Amalfi MB-Viper and he would covet it. That is until he saw his boring, predictable ex-wife draped over it, swathed in silk and diamonds.

After their marriage, his affair with another nurse at the hospital where Annabelle had been finishing up her nursing degree had left her feeling like her soul had been murdered.

A chance meeting with Mel, who'd been one of the heart patients on her floor at the time, had resulted in her going to work for him. His job offer had spirited her away from a world of pain she'd wanted to put behind her and hopefully forget.

Now Guilio's faith in her being attractive enough to grace his ads gave her another shot of confidence her damaged self-esteem had been needing.

"You will stay at my home with my wife, Maria, and me. I'm eager to introduce you to my brothers and my two married stepsons, who work for me. They and their families live nearby."

"I'd love to meet all of them, but I couldn't impose on you and your wife that way."

"Hmm. I can see you're stubborn like my son. All right. I'll put you up in Ravello's finest hotel."

"No hotel. If I'm going to be in Italy, I want to stay in some quaint, modest bed-and-breakfast where it's quiet, away from people and I can soak in the atmosphere. Here in Los Angeles we're constantly hemmed in by each other."

He turned to Mel. "You won't mind loaning her to me? This is business."

Mel smiled. "Not if you send her back soon. I couldn't get along without her. She's the reason I haven't had another heart attack."

Guilio smacked his own head. "*Cielo!* We don't want that."

All three of them had laughed.

Eight weeks ago she'd agreed to model for him and now, having completed her first four days of work in Rome, she found herself transported to Ravello, home to the Cavezzali family and the Amalfi car, a design as spectacular as the Amalfi coast itself.

Perched high above the water, Ravello was more like a giant garden than a town. Guilio, who had his own villas here, called it the crown jewel of the Sorrentine Peninsula. Princes, movies stars and sheikhs, among others, were drawn to the cluster of colorful cliff side villages and sparkling harbors dotting the world-famous stretch of Italian coastline.

This was her first vacation since her honeymoon to Mexico four years ago. After telling Guilio she wanted to stay in one of those charming little Italian farm-houses like she'd seen in films and on television, the kind that made you dream about the countryside, he'd installed her here.

She'd learned this house sat on the little farm his first wife had left to his son Lucca. It had stood vacant for fifteen years. She was welcome to stay here.

The exterior was orangy-pink with jade shutters. The only door to the house was on the side and led into the kitchen. Pure enchantment. Since leaving the bustle of Rome earlier in the day, nothing could have delighted her more.

While its terrace overlooked the brilliant blue Tyrrhenian Sea, an explosion of white daisies reached for the sky and pushed their way through the bars of the railing. It was as if the house had been planted inside a basket of blossoms. She couldn't wait to go exploring the area in the morning, before her driver came by for her at eleven.

After taking off her clothes, she stepped in the shower. It felt good to wash her hair and emerge later feeling fresh and clean after traveling most of the day.

She threw on her well-worn navy robe and plugged in the adaptor before turning on the blow dryer. When the strands weren't quite as damp, she pinned them to the top of her head. Tomorrow the hairdresser would decide what he wanted to do with her shoulder-length hair for the photo shoot.

Another glance in the mirror proved that the Amalfi Girl was gone for the night.

Was twenty-six still young enough for her to be called a girl? Did her daily makeover at the hands of experts hide the traces of the betrayed widow? The camera would tell the truth, but Guilio believed in what he was doing. He believed in her. She already cared for him so much, she wanted this campaign to be a huge success and was determined to cooperate every way she could.

When Lucca learned what his father had done in his honor, he'd be touched beyond belief. It was very sweet really. Guilio was about as excited as a father who'd put his child's most wanted gift under the Christmas tree and couldn't wait for him to open it.

Unfortunately it was only June. Annabelle wondered how he was going to be able to wait until August when the car was finally out in the showrooms. The timing would coincide with his son's next leave and the grand unveiling would take place in Milan.

Guilio intended to fly her back over for the special event, which would be covered by Italian television and other media sources. "We'll do a blitz!" Guilio proclaimed with excitement. "Nothing's too good for my Lucca."

Annabelle imagined his bachelor son had the same Cavezzali drive and charm. She admitted to a growing curiosity about him. Guilio had told her the den at his villa was full of pictures showing his son at every stage of his life. The latest ones showed Lucca receiving commendations and ribbons. She was eager to see them along with everything else.

After stretching her arms, she smiled wryly to herself, still unable to believe that she was in the most glorious place on earth, enjoying a free vacation while she modeled, and having the time of her life. In a few weeks she would have to go home, but she refused to think about that right now.

Once she'd brushed her teeth, she turned out the light and padded down the beamed hall to the larger of the two bedrooms made ready for her. The cozy feel of the old house, which was filled with old family pictures and furnishings, enveloped her. So many stories these fieldstone walls would tell if they could speak.

Annabelle climbed under the covers of the double bed. With a sigh she sank back against the pillow and closed her eyes, more tired than she realized. On such a beautiful June night, she wished she could leave the windows open, but Guilio had warned her against it.

"You can't ever be too careful."

Annabelle knew he was right.

"Tomorrow after the shoot, I'll give you a car so you can come and go as you please."

"Thank you for everything, Guilio. I guess you know you've brought me to heaven."

"Ravello is the closest thing to it. Call me if you need anything. Sleep well, Annabelle. *Ciao.*"

"*Ciao.*"

She didn't know why, but as she nestled into a more comfortable position, she had a feeling that love and laughter had filled this house years ago. Some marriages lasted. Her eyes misted. How nice for those lucky people...

At the base of the tiny farm bordering the serpentine road, Lucca Cavezzali got an urge to go on foot from here and told the driver he'd hired to stop the car. After paying the man, he got out of the backseat with some difficulty and reached for his duffel bag.

There was a full moon overhead. Anyone up at two in the morning would see him and wonder who was trespassing on private property. He took a long look around. In the next instant the perfumed breeze brought back memories from the past. The scent of orange blossoms hung heavily in the air, recalling his childhood, which had been idyllic when his mother had been alive.

After her death, everything changed. Lucca had watched his father turn into a different man, who soon after her death married a widow with two sons. At fourteen years of age Lucca couldn't forgive him for that and pretty well closed up on him.

Uninterested in going into the family car business like his stepbrothers and cousins, he'd left to join the military at eighteen. His grandfather Lorenzo had served in the Second World War. Lucca had made the old farmer out to be a hero and had romanticized about going off to war himself.

That decision had caused a serious rift between him and Guilio, who raged that Lucca might not be as lucky as his grandfather and not make it back at all. Still, nothing had dissuaded Lucca from leaving. But as he grew into a man and had firsthand knowledge of what war was really like, understanding of a lot of things caught up to him, like his father's fears for his only son's safety, and Guilio's need for love and companionship after losing Lucca's mother.

Lucca had long since let go of his teenage hang-ups. Over the years he'd mended the breech between them and had come to like his stepmother. She'd been good for his father, who was married to his work building up the Amalfi car industry.

If there was anything left over from the past, it was his guilt for not having been around the last fifteen years for his father. But the hospital psychiatrist had worked through those issues with him as well as his survivor's guilt. The doctor had told him most career servicemen and women suffered the same problems. Guilt went with the territory.

The only issue that Lucca didn't want to see turn into a problem had arisen on his last leave. He'd found out his father was considering selling off the two remaining farm properties from his mother's side of the family that were in sore need of care. Lucca had immediately made an offer for them.

His father looked at him as if he were crazy. If Lucca wanted to build up some investments, it would be a better use of his money to buy a prime piece of business real estate in town. Guilio was a shrewd businessman and considered his opinion to be the final word on the subject.

Rather than get into a full-blown argument as they'd done too often in those early years, Lucca decided to leave it alone for the time being. All he asked was that his father not do anything about the properties until he came home on his next leave in August, when they had more time for a business discussion.

But since their last meeting, he'd undergone a life-changing experience that had altered his timetable.

Four months ago Lucca had been shot down and it had ended his military career. Guilio didn't know about the crash that had left Lucca permanently injured, or that he'd been in the hospital all this time.

Aware how his father would have suffered for him had he known about the operation on his leg and the long rehabilitation, not to mention his post-traumatic stress disorder, Lucca made certain no news had leaked out from his superiors or doctors. It was a time he preferred to forget.

Tomorrow he would show up at his father's house after a good night's sleep. That's when he had less pain. He wanted to feel rested when he told Guilio about his future plans to be a full-time farmer. It was possible he'd meet with the same negative reaction of years ago, but Lucca had to try.

Before turning eighteen, Lucca had talked to his father and told him that he wanted to be a farmer, but Guilio had thrown up his hands. "For your mother's family, farming was fine. But no son of mine is going to do that kind of work! You're a Cavezzali with a superior brain!

"Our family has been designing and manufacturing cars since World War Two. There's no distinction in being a farmer who's always subject to the elements and works all hours of the day and night with little to show for it. No, Lucca. You listen to your father!"

After Guilio's tirade, Lucca kept the dream to himself. Instead of joining the Amalfi car business after graduation, he went into the military. Not to spite his father, but because he had plans to be a farmer one day and that ambition meant he would have to make some real money at a job that appealed to him first. Being a fighter pilot satisfied that need.

Now that he was out of the service, he planned to work with the soil and revive the farm. Since he intended to be successful and make a substantial profit, he needed more parcels of land. Along with this farm and those two properties to which he'd always been sentimentally attached, he could make a good start and go from there.

He'd had a lot of time to think in the hospital and hoped that when he talked to his father, Guilio's opinions would have softened enough to really listen to Lucca. But he doubted his father would ever approve of what he intended to do. Already Lucca was bracing for the same kind of lecture his father had given him all that time ago.

However, this time Lucca wouldn't be dissuaded and he wasn't going away. And if his father chose not to sell the properties, then Lucca was prepared to buy others. After his inactivity these last four months, he ached to get busy using his hands.

Once he'd checked his watch, he started for the house, struggling to reach it with every step. Before the injury that could have taken off his leg, he would have ambled up the steep incline between the orange and lemon trees faster than any goat.

As he made his way over uneven ground, he noted with disgust that everything growing required attention and pruning. The whole place needed an overhaul. Weeds fought to displace the flowers growing in wild profusion around the base of the deserted house, particularly in front of the terrace, where the railing was almost invisible. So much work needed to be done.

If his mother were alive, she would weep to see the neglect. Maybe it was just as well he'd lost her in his early teens. That way she wasn't here to see him come home a wreck of a man. Thirty-three years old and he wasn't a pretty sight. Neither was the farm, but he was about to change all that, with or without his father's blessing.

Working his way around the side to the only door leading into the house, he pulled out a set of keys and let himself in. Usually when he had a furlough, he met his father in Rome or Milan, where Guilio often did business at the major showrooms. But those days were over.

He was back on the farm, his own small piece of heaven, and he planned to work it.

From what Lucca could tell, there didn't appear to be any dust. He'd been paying a local woman to make sure the place was cleaned on a periodic basis and was pleased to see she'd followed through. He put the duffel bag down on the tiles in the kitchen with relief. It weighed a ton.

No longer encumbered, he limped past the small table and chairs to the hallway, taking in the living room on the other side. He didn't need lights turned on to find his old bedroom. Everything was still in place, like a time capsule that had just been opened.

He moved over to the window and undid the shutters, letting in the sound of the cicadas. Moonlight poured in, illuminating the double bed minus any bedding. Unlatching the glass, he pushed it all the way open to allow the scented breeze to dance on through. There was no other air like it anywhere on earth. He knew, because he'd been everywhere.

While he stood there filling his lungs with the sweet essence of the fruits and flowers, the pain in his leg grew worse. The plate the surgeon had put in his thigh to support the broken bone caused it to ache when he was tired. He needed another painkiller followed by sleep. A long one.

*Diavolo!* It meant going back to the kitchen, but he didn't know if he could make it without help. Walking the distance from the car had exhausted him.

Somewhere in his closet among his favorite treasures he remembered his grandfather's cane. His mother's father had lost the lower half of his leg in the war and had eventually been fitted with a prosthesis.

He rummaged around inside until he spotted it, never dreaming the day would come when he would find use for it. *Grazie a Dio* Lucca hadn't lost a limb.

Armed with the precious heirloom, he left the bedroom and headed for the kitchen, where he'd put the duffel bag. He'd packed the pill bottle in his shaving kit on top. Once he'd swallowed painkillers, he ran the tap water, then lowered his head and drank his fill. It tasted good.

He eventually shut off the tap. One more stop to the bathroom before sinking into oblivion.

By now he was leaning heavily on the cane. The short climb to the house had done its damage. Only a few more feet… *Come on. You can do it!* But even as he said the words, the cane slid on the tiles from his weight and he went crashing.

A loud thump resounded in the hallway followed by a yelp and a volley of unintelligible cursing in Italian. Annabelle shot up in bed. Someone—a man—was in the house, thrashing about after some kind of fall. It couldn't be Guilio. He would have phoned if he'd intended to come over for some reason. Maybe it was the caretaker Guilio had forgotten to tell her about.

With her heart in her throat, she slid out of bed. After throwing on her robe, she hurried over to the door. When she opened it, enough moonlight spilled from the doorway of the other bedroom to outline a figure crawling on his hands and knees.

Knowing the intruder was hurt in some way, she felt braver as she found the switch in the hall and turned on the light. His dark head reared back in complete surprise, revealing a striking face riddled with lines of pain. She grabbed for the cane she could see lying a few feet from him and lifted it in the air.

"I don't know who you are," she said through clenched teeth. "You probably don't speak English, but I'm warning you I'll use this if you make another move." With a threatening gesture, she took a step toward him.

"You have me at a disadvantage, *signorina*."

His deep voice spoke beautiful English with the kind of Italian accent that resonated to her insides. He was probably in his mid-thirties. The dangerous-looking male didn't have the decency to flinch. Even on the floor twisting in agony, he exuded an air of authority. She doubted he was anyone's caretaker. This kindled her fear of his lean, hard-muscled body on a level she didn't wish to examine.

"You're trespassing on private property, *signore*."

He strained to brace his back against the wall. A black T-shirt covered his well-defined chest. With his legs stretched out full length in jeans molding powerful thighs, she could see he would be six-two or six-three if he were standing. He put her in mind of someone, but she couldn't think who.

"You took the words out of my mouth, *signorina*. A man has the right to come home to his own house and be alone."

She drew in a fortifying breath. "I happen to know that no one has lived in this house for years."

His lids drooped over his eyes. He was exhausted. Perspiration beaded his forehead and upper lip. She saw the signs of his pain and felt unwanted sympathy for his distress, but it only lasted until he said, "Nevertheless it's mine, so what are you doing here?"

"*You're* the intruder," she snapped. "I'll ask the questions if you don't mind. First of all, I want to see your ID."

"I don't have it on me."

"Of course you don't."

"It's in the kitchen."

"Of course it is," she mocked again. "And if I ask for your name, you'll lie to me, so there's no point. We'll let the police get the truth out of you."

That made him open his eyes enough to gaze up at her through inky black lashes. "How sad your cynicism is already showing."

Heat made its way into her cheeks. "Already?"

"Well, for one thing you're not married." He stared at her ringless fingers. "Disillusionment doesn't usually happen to a woman until she's approaching forty. At least that's been my assessment."

He'd pressed the wrong button. "It would take a broken-down, forty-year-old cynic of a man to know, wouldn't it? Your vast knowledge on the subject doesn't seem to have done you a whole lot of good. No wedding ring on your finger, either. Not even the paler ring of skin to give proof you'd once worn one. What you need is a walker that won't slip, *signore*, not a cane."

The lines around his mouth tightened. She didn't know if she'd hit her target, or if he was reacting to his pain.

He slanted her an impatient glance. "Why don't you admit you're a down-and-out tourist who doesn't have enough money for a hotel room, so you cased the area and settled on this empty house."

Smarting from the accusation she said, "What if I were? You've done the same thing by waiting until the middle of the night to find a vacant spot to lick your wounds."

"Like a stray dog, you mean?"

Behind his snarl-like question she heard a bleakness that matched the whitish color around his lips. They'd traded insults long enough. His pain caused her to relent. "I'm a guest here for a time. My name is Annabelle Marsh. What's yours?"

He rested his head of unruly black hair against the wall. "None of your business" was the off-putting response.

His eyes had closed, giving her enough time to hurry into the bedroom and grab her cell phone off the side table. When she returned seconds later, his lids fluttered open. "What do you think you're doing?" he demanded curtly.

"I'm calling Guilio Cavezzali, my employer. He'll know how to deal with you."

"No, don't—" He lunged forward and pulled her down, cradling her between his legs with great strength.

The gesture sent the cane flying down the hall. His hands tore the cell phone from her other hand. It slid even farther away. She felt his warm breath on her nape. "I can't let you call him at this hour."

Did he know Guilio? The name seemed to mean something to him. Annabelle had been a fool to feel any pity for him. Now she was at his mercy. She schooled her voice to remain steady. "What is it you want?"

"Invisibility for the rest of the night. One word from you could ruin everything."

"I guess if you were being hunted by the police you wouldn't tell me, or maybe you would and don't care."

He made a strange sound in his throat. "I'm not on anyone's suspect list. More to the point, how long have you been staying here?"

She could feel the pounding of his heart against her back. It was too fast. His pain would have spiked from the sudden exertion. "I only arrived in Ravello this evening." In her own way, she'd wanted invisibility after a full day.

"How soon will you be seeing him again?"

"He'll be sending a car for me tomorrow at eleven. I'll probably see him later in the day."

"What exactly do you do?"

This man who'd broken into the house seemed to know more than she'd given him credit for, but she wasn't about to reveal information about Guilio. Seeing as this stranger had her locked in his grip, he had the upper hand. What choice was there except to answer with as much truth as she dared and still protect Guilio. His name was synonymous with Amalfi and prominent throughout Italy. "I'm working for him temporarily."

"Why aren't you living in a *pensione* or an apartment?" The man was full of questions.

"I asked him to find me a farmhouse that rented out rooms. That's when he told me I could stay here. There's no place more beautiful than the Italian countryside. Living here is like walking right into the picture on a calendar of Italy and never wanting to come back out."

"That's very interesting." He'd said the words, but he didn't sound as if he believed her.

She breathed in sharply. "Now that that I've answered all of your questions, it's only fair you answer one for me. Who *are* you?"

"Lucca Cavezzali," he groaned.

"Oh, no—" she cried. This was Guilio's only son, the adored child he'd had with his first wife, the eighteen-year-old who'd gone into the military and had trained to be a fighter pilot for the Italian air force—his father's pride and joy!

If she told him the specific nature of her job, it would ruin the surprise his father had been planning for over a year.

Now that she thought about it, the two men had similar builds, though Guilio was shorter. She saw a vague resemblance in some of their facial features, but Lucca must have inherited his black hair from his mother. Guilio hadn't mentioned anything about his son being injured.

She tried to get away from him, but he held her firmly against him. "Because of you, *signorina*, my best laid plans have been shot to hell for tonight, as you Americans like to say."

"You're right! We *do* like to say," she spluttered back. "Allow me to thank you very much, *signore*. Your unexpected, unforetold nocturnal invasion has changed *my* plans, too. If you'll let me go, I'll phone for a taxi and be gone from here inside of a half hour."

To her dismay she would have to explain to Guilio why she'd suddenly decided to go to a hotel after all. She would have to think up a good excuse for leaving, but she'd worry about that later.

"Now who's licking wounds," he muttered with uncanny perception.

"That's none of *your* business."

"I'm afraid it is. But uprooting you tonight won't be necessary, provided you're willing to cooperate with me and keep my presence here a secret until tomorrow."

*Cooperate?* For the second time that night she was suffering fresh shock after learning his identity. "You ask a lot of your prisoners." She'd been trying to wiggle free from his viselike grip, but it was no use. He might be injured, but he was incredibly strong and fit.

"I'm a desperate man."

Annabelle moaned. "So I've noticed. Why don't you want your father to know you're back?"

"Back from where, *signorina*?"

His condescending tone told her that no matter what she said, he wasn't going to like it. "He mentioned that you're in the military." She moistened her lips nervously. "Did you arrange for a special leave or something?"

"That's not your affair, either."

She supposed it wasn't. "You're right, but I can tell you're in pain. You should be in bed."

"I was on my way there." He'd come from the other part of the house, probably the kitchen. His speech had slowed, leading her to believe he'd drugged himself with something strong.

"Your bed isn't made up. You'll have to use mine."

"As long as you don't leave my sight. For the rest of the night we'll lie on the same bed to ensure you don't play the informer before morning."

Annabelle had no illusions. That was a command, not an invitation. She refused to react. "Fine. If you'll let me stand, I'll help you get up, then you can lean on me. My bedroom isn't far."

He let her go with one hand, using it to brace himself against the wall while he clung to her arm with the other. She sensed he would have cried out if he'd been alone. Together they moved to her bedroom with him leaning on her. Undoubtedly she would have collapsed from his weight if they'd had to go much farther.

By some miracle they made it to the bed. He fell on his side, taking her with him. She ended up on her back and felt his hand curl around her wrist, making certain she wouldn't get away. As he settled against the pillows, his sigh of relief echoed off the walls of the room.

When she'd helped him up moments ago, the dark stubble on his jaw had brushed against her cheek by accident, reminding her of his undeniable masculinity. No doubt he'd been traveling a long time without stopping to freshen up. Between fatigue and the medication he'd taken for his pain, she assumed he'd be asleep before long.

She, on the other hand, lay next to him, wide-awake. There'd been no man since she'd divorced Ryan. With Guilio's son facing her inches away, her senses were in chaos. The situation was so surreal she wondered if she were dreaming.

"Don't be afraid," Lucca murmured, thinking he'd read her mind. "I couldn't take advantage of you if I wanted to, which I don't."

His words might have pricked her if she hadn't already been through a hell she never wanted to repeat. "Then we're both in luck because I can assure you that a rude, brooding, unshaven male slithering home under cover of darkness is no woman's idea of joy beyond measure." His earlier remarks still smarted.

He made a sound that bordered on angry laughter, but none of it mattered. In another few minutes he'd be dead to the world. Once his hand released her, she would find some clean bedding in the hall closet and make up the other bed.

"Your pillow smells of strawberries."

The observation came as a surprise. In fact everything he said and did had knocked her off balance. "It's probably still damp, too. I'll get you another one."

His hand restrained her from moving. "After the places I've been, I like it." The words came out in a slur.

"You can let go of me. I'm not going to reveal your secret."

"Why not?" came the unexpected question "It's the kind of thing a woman can't wait to do."

If he could still try to rile her, then he wasn't as close to sleep as she'd supposed. Probably because of his pain. She fought an unwanted rush of sympathy for him. "That kind of assumption comes from knowing too many females on a superficial basis."

"You're an authority on my love life now?" he growled.

"Italian men have a certain reputation, *signore*. As we American women understand it, the Italian male is a jack of all trades, but master of none. I think it's one of the personal casualties in your particular line of work."

To his credit he let her baiting go before he said in a raspy voice, "You still haven't answered my question."

For the most important of reasons. She happened to know that Lucca's next furlough wasn't scheduled until August when he visited with his father in Milan. The big surprise Guilio was planning for him would take place at the largest Amalfi showroom in Italy. From there the cars were manufactured and exported around the world.

Annabelle remembered the look in Guilio's eyes as he'd talked about wanting to honor Lucca when they met at the end of the summer. She would never spoil that reunion by revealing ahead of time what she knew he had in store for his son.

Exhausted over the stunning events of the last hour, her eyelids closed. "If I haven't responded, it's because anyone who has gone to your lengths to sneak back under the radar in the dead of night must have the kind of baggage he wouldn't want anyone to know about."

She felt his body stiffen.

"What do you say we both try to get some sleep, *signore*? I don't know about you, but I have a big day tomorrow."

"You've got me intrigued about the nature of the work you do for my father. It must be beyond classified, otherwise he wouldn't be treating you like a princess. Nor would he have installed you in a house that is sacrosanct to me." His voice suddenly sounded as if it had come from a deep cavern.

The blood started pounding in her ears. "Sacrosanct?" she whispered.

"You mean he didn't tell you I was born here? Would it surprise you to know my mother died in this house?"

*Oh, no.*

To think she'd called *him* the intruder. "Your father only told me your mother willed this farm to you. I didn't realize about the house."

"Let's just say he has kept an eye on it for me."

# CHAPTER TWO

A DULL throbbing ache woke Lucca. It radiated up his thigh to his groin. His medication had worn off. He needed some more quick before the pain flared out of control, as it had done last night.

Last night…

He rubbed a hand over his prickly jaws, groaning in self-disgust.

Sunlight filled the room, forcing him to squint. He checked his watch. Twenty to eleven. He found himself alone, still dressed in the same clothes minus his shoes, which she'd removed. The bed was in total disarray, evidence he'd had one of his nightmares. The quilt and pillows lay on the floor.

Naturally she was long gone. By now the American would have alerted his father, who had her allegiance. Lucca was sure he could expect a visitor shortly.

A spate of Italian invective poured out of him.

He turned slowly to roll off the mattress and gave a start to see his near-empty bottle of pills on the bed-side table. It hadn't been there last night. She'd even supplied a glass of water. On the other side of the lamp lay the cane. He decided the nurses at the hospital had nothing on her. His father required efficiency. She had that trait down pat.

Lucca had planned on total privacy for one night, but he had to admit that being this close to his pills meant he didn't need to suffer another accident on the way to the kitchen.

After swallowing three, his stomach growled, reminding him he hadn't eaten since yesterday afternoon on the last leg of his flight to Naples. During the long wait for the train to Salerno, sleep had been impossible. The lack of it always increased the pain. By the time he'd hired a car to drive him to Ravello, he'd been ready to collapse.

A quick scan of the room revealed none of her belongings. He heard no noise and imagined the car she'd mentioned had already come for her. Alone at last, he got up from the bed and tested his weight with the cane. Last night's accident had been an aberration. As long as he didn't lean on it too heavily, the cane would do fine until he'd recovered.

The trip from the bathroom to the kitchen wasn't too bad. His duffel bag was still on the floor where he'd left it. It looked untouched.

He opened the fridge and found it stocked. This house had belonged to his mother's family. She and his father had lived in it until she'd died. In the will, she'd left the house and property to Lucca. At the time he'd joined the military, he and his father weren't speaking, but he knew Guilio would keep an eye on it.

How strange he'd decided to install his new American employee here. Even though she'd claimed she wanted to stay at a farmhouse, his father wouldn't have gone to the trouble to open up the house where he'd started out his married life for just any person working for him. This woman had to occupy a unique place in the scheme of things.

That's why she hadn't opened up to him last night. She and his father had something private going on. He had to admit she'd recovered fast from her fright last night. His interrogation of her proved she was a quick study.

Naturally Guilio would have sent down one of the maids from the villa to make sure things were ready for her. He reached for a handful of fat grapes from a bowl and popped them in his mouth. Their juice squirted pure sugar.

The microwave was new. His father had set her up with the necessities. A jar of freeze-dried coffee stood next to it. He preferred *cappuccino chiaro*, but in the military he'd learned to drink it black and made himself a cup.

In his line of vision to the terrace he noticed several branches from one of the lemon trees had grown and formed an overhang. While he leaned against the sink to sip the hot brew, he saw movement beneath them. Beyond the French doors he watched the back of a woman of medium height picking daisies near the half-hidden railing.

Her hair was caught beneath a large, broad-rimmed straw hat. The rest of her was dressed in a sleeveless white top trimmed with a small white eyelet ruffle. Equally immaculate white pants skimmed womanly hips down to the bone-colored sandals on her feet, where he glimpsed frosted pink toenails.

He waited until she turned enough for him to see the classic profile of *Signorina* Marsh. So she hadn't gone off early… Last night her bathrobe had covered up her slender curves.

The whiteness of her fresh-looking outfit combined with the profusion of white petals drew his gaze. With that face partially hidden beneath the hat rim and set against a backdrop of blue sky melding into cobalt waters far below, it was like beholding one of those picture-perfect postcards in dazzling Technicolor.

As she came in through the unlocked doors bringing the sunshine with her, her eyes lit on him, but she kept going and put the flowers in a ceramic pitcher on the counter. After filling it with water, she placed it in the center of the rectangular kitchen table, which was inlaid with hand-painted tiles of lemons.

His mother used to bring in fresh flowers in the early morning. He experienced a moment's resentment to be reminded of happier times that would never come again.

"I've always wanted to be able to decorate with flowers from my own garden. These are for me, but enjoy them if you want to. They're glorious." Dusting off her hands, she reached for a large straw handbag lying on one of the chairs and walked over to the side door.

With a parting glance from eyes a rare shade of periwinkle she added, "My ride will be arriving any minute. I'm going to walk out to the drive so you can remain invisible." She started to open the door, then paused.

"Please wipe that morose expression off your face. You're probably not that bad-looking when you aren't carrying the world around on your shoulders like Atlas. Surely you realize I didn't mean the things I said last night."

"Only half," he muttered in an acerbic tone after finishing the rest of his coffee.

"Hmm, maybe three quarters. When you make yourself another cup of coffee, there's sugar in the cupboard. I'd say you needed a little sweetening. Before I leave, tell me the truth. How recently were you released from the hospital?"

His lips twisted unpleasantly. "What hospital would that be?" He opened the fridge and found a plum to bite into.

"The one where you had surgery on your right thigh. You're favoring your other leg and can't get into any one comfortable position for long."

He munched until there was nothing left but the pit, which he removed and tossed in the wastebasket in the corner. "You're mistaken, *signorina*."

"No." Annabelle remained firm. "The medication you're taking tells me otherwise."

On cue his dark brows furrowed with menace. "What makes you such an authority?"

"I'm a nurse with experience taking care of patients recovering from heart and thoracic surgery, gunshot wounds, broken bones."

Stillness surrounded him before she saw a look of alarm break out on his face. "What's wrong with my father?"

She blinked, trying to make sense of his hyperspeed leap from the subject at hand to Guilio. Once the light dawned, she cried, "No, no— I'm not working for your father in that capacity. I'm helping do some advertising for him. As far as I know, he's fine!" she assured him, noting that his first reaction had been one of a son who loved his father. That cleared up one question haunting her.

His eyes looked disbelieving.

"*You're* the person I'm worried about, *signore*. I've a feeling you left the hospital before it was wise. Combined with the fall you had last night, you need to nurse that leg as much as possible. Even if the pain has subsided for now, you're wiped out."

"*Grazie* for your concern."

She decided the ice between them was thawing a few degrees. His sarcasm didn't come off sounding quite as bitter as before. "*Prego*." It was one of few words she knew in Italian for *you're welcome*.

"*One* more thing, *signore*. I told Guilio I didn't want any maids or housekeepers around while I'm here, so you should have no worries in that department. After work I'll be back to pack and go to a hotel. I don't know the exact time of my arrival, but rest assured I'll be alone," she promised with a pleasant expression.

He watched her disappear out the side door. If she could be believed, then he had little to worry about for the rest of the day. But it caused him to wonder that she'd be willing to keep his secret that long.

Why would she do it? For how long? She wanted something in return, evidently enough to be willing to cooperate.

Breaking in on a defenseless woman in the dead of night should have scared her senseless. Instead, she'd turned the tables on him and had made threatening gestures with the cane. He felt a grudging admiration for her resourcefulness. But he couldn't help but question what she expected to gain by her compliance with Lucca's wishes. Did she think getting on his good side would earn her a promotion with his father down the road? More perks?

What was his father playing at? To let his alleged

employee have her own way and install her in Lucca's house meant she'd twisted him around her finger. What kind of advertising was she doing for his father?

It was a little late for him to be having a midlife crisis. Surely his second wife—Maria was enough for him. She'd managed to marry him only six months after Lucca's mother had been buried. For years Lucca had blamed her for changing his father. Until one day when Lucca grew up and realized no force could make Guilio marry the attractive widow who had two sons of her own if he hadn't wanted to.

Now this American woman—a nurse, no less—had come into Guilio's life, so different in every way that Lucca was baffled.

He frowned. Nine months ago when he'd flown to Milan on furlough for a brief visit to see his father, *Signorina* Marsh hadn't been on the payroll. That meant she was a fairly recent addition to the company, but because she was in his father's confidence, she had Lucca at a disadvantage.

He didn't like the idea that she would know more about him than he wanted anyone to know, yet for the time being he had no choice but to live with it. It didn't escape him that he bore some responsibility for arriving in the dead of night.

After locking the door, he turned to the fridge. While he rummaged for items to fix himself a sandwich, he heard a car turn into the gravel drive. The voices were too faint for him to make out conversation. Before long it drove off.

In a minute he sank down on one of the hand-carved wooden chairs. He extended his long legs, trying to get into a more comfortable position, which was virtually impossible, just like she'd said. As he bit into some locally grown ham and his favorite *provolone dolce* cheese, he found himself glowering at the daisies she'd put in the old family pitcher and hardly noticed the taste.

He'd wanted complete solitude and sleep for one night. That way he could appear at his father's door today looking rested enough that Guilio's first reaction wouldn't be one of heartache over his son. There'd been enough of that in the early days.

Soon enough his father would learn about the flash-backs, but they usually happened after he fell asleep.

Starting to get that drugged feeling, he headed for the bedroom. Whether *Signorina* Marsh exposed him or not, he was no longer alone in his own home and wouldn't be able to totally relax.

He should phone his father right now, but the pain since his fall last night was more than he could bear right now. Once the pills took effect, he would pass out again for a few hours. When he awakened, he had to pray the throbbing would have died down enough that he could make the call.

Annabelle stepped out of the van where they'd done her hair and makeup. "*Perfetto, signorina*. That's the look I want. Like a *margheritina*!"

"What is that?"

"A flower." Giovanni, the photographer, put one of his hands on top of the other and made spokes.

"Ah. A wheel. You mean like, he loves me, he loves me not?"

He grinned. "*Sì, Sì.*"

Annabelle didn't mind being compared to a daisy. Not at all. The beautiful ones she'd picked earlier that morning had called to her. She'd experienced a euphoric moment until she'd gone back in the kitchen and found the dark Italian owner scrutinizing her with all the intensity of his brooding soul. She wished she still didn't quake when she thought about it.

Meeting him in the flesh in the middle of the night had, to some extent, altered her vision of the picture his father had portrayed of a strong, powerful man. But obviously that was her fault for endowing his hero son with certain admirable virtues. Maybe his good qualities were there, but they were disguised by pain and his participation in a war where no one ever came home the same as before they left.

She admitted to being worried about his insistence on not letting his father know he was back yet. Though it wasn't any of her business, as Lucca had said, she *did* care. More than she should. It made her impatient with herself.

"Annabelle?"

Her head jerked up. "Yes?"

The shorter, overweight man Basilio—one of Guilio's assistants, who'd driven her this morning—provided the interpretation for the pose he had in mind. "We want you to get in the driver's seat now and lean to the passenger side, putting your right arm here. Remember you're out beneath a midafternoon sun, driving for the sheer thrill of it. Then you see the water below and you have to pull over to get a better view. React the way you would naturally. Forget the camera."

Easy for *him* to say. But this was an adventure she wouldn't have missed.

Without needing more urging, Annabelle climbed in the black Amalfi convertible. She could almost believe this was Mrs. James Bond's car. The rich black-leather interior provided the ideal foil for the white outfit she'd put on before leaving the farmhouse. So far she couldn't fault Marcella's superb fashion taste.

Annabelle couldn't decide which sports car she liked better. The other one in Rome parked in front of the fighter jet had been white with light pearl-grey leather. Lucca would look sensational speeding around in either of them, but the thrill probably wouldn't be the same after the years he'd flown above the clouds at super-sonic speeds.

Once she'd gotten into her role, Giovanni put the straw hat back on her head, studying the angle for a minute and doing a rearrangement of her hair before he started taking one picture after another.

The car had been parked next to the wall of the steep highway below Positano. When she looked down, she gasped at the sheer drop to the water, forgetting every-thing else. Such gorgeous scenery—reputed to be the most fantastic in this part of the world—defied verbal description and became a spiritual experience with na-ture. This kind of beauty actually hurt.

With the help of the police, hundreds of cars going both ways had to pass single file where the photo shoot was taking place. Though there were a few angry shouts and horn honks, by far more tourists whistled and shouted *"squisitas"* and *"bellissimas"*, throwing her kisses as they passed by.

Yet the view was too mesmerizing and she was barely cognizant of anything else going on around her. If the truth be told, her mind was preoccupied with an image of the wounded Italian pilot who'd finally fallen asleep last night, relaxing his hold so she could escape. Talk about a beautiful man...

When Giovanni announced he had all the shots he needed, she hurried back to the van to remove her makeup. She'd brought her own change of clothes in the straw bag and quickly slipped on her jeans and a blouse. Once she was dressed, she left everything else in the van and stepped outside clutching her own purse.

Besides the sports car and the van, there was the third car Basilio had driven when he'd picked her up at the farm. It was an older model blue Amalfi sedan. He gave her the key, telling her it was now hers to use while she was in Italy.

The police directing traffic indicated they needed to get rid of the roadblock as fast as possible. With the agreement that she'd meet the film crew tomorrow at noon in the town of Amalfi for another photo shoot, she got in the car and followed the policeman riding a motorcycle out into the stream of cars. He helped her get her place in line with the other vehicles headed back toward Ravello.

Through the rearview mirror she saw him blow her a kiss. Annabelle smiled. Italian men. Always open in their enjoyment of women. They were hilarious. Except for one Lucca Cavezzali. She frowned, needing to arm herself ahead of time for a dour reception from him once she returned.

She'd seen his bottle of pills. He was almost out of them. They were the strongest painkillers one could take after surgery without going back to the hospital for a morphine cocktail. His fall in the hallway last night had been doubly unfortunate for him. It came from returning home the hard way, but it *was* his call after all, and his house. The injured man had every right to expect it would be empty.

Before she arrived at the farmhouse, she made two stops on the outskirts of Ravello. One to a pizzeria for a light meal. The other to a *gelateria* that was a few doors down from a charming-looking bed-and-breakfast. She checked it out and found out there was a vacancy. With easy access to the main road, she couldn't find anything better and held the room with a credit card for two weeks occupancy.

Now that Lucca was back home, she couldn't stay at the farmhouse and would check in after she'd gone back to pack. While she ate a delicious lemon ice, she returned her parents' phone call, letting them know she'd left Rome and was now settled in Ravello.

Considering the time difference between Italy and California, they'd already gone to work some time ago, so she left her message on their answering machine. Being the last of three children, she knew they worried about her and wanted her to be happy. The prerogative of parents.

A familiar ache passed through Annabelle because the experience of having a baby had been denied her. But then she quickly brightened, refusing to dwell on it, and assured her folks she was having a wonderful time. How could she not after the sights she'd seen today.

She left out mention of the owner of the farmhouse, who'd come close to giving her a heart attack last night when he'd decided to come home without telling his father. Guilio worshipped his son, but clearly there was some history between them that caused Lucca to hold back.

Annabelle didn't pretend to understand the family

dynamics known only to the two of them, but she respected them. Nothing could be worse for her than to be caught smack-dab in the middle of father-and-son issues.

Whatever Lucca decided to do or not do, tomorrow she would tell Guilio that the farmhouse was too isolated after all and she'd found a place with eating establishments next door that suited her. She wanted out of this precarious situation. It was up to Lucca to contact his father. He'd had a day to think about it.

A minute later she pulled into the drive at the side of the farmhouse and parked the car.

Twilight was fast fading into darkness. Combined with the soft, fragrant air, it was a magical time of night. But when she opened the door to the kitchen, reality intruded because she was met by a man holding on to the kitchen counter. His facial features were taut with pain. Even his knuckles were white.

Without thinking she said, "You need to go to an emergency room."

"What I need are more pills," he corrected in a gravelly voice.

"Why in heaven's name didn't you phone your father?"

"My original plan had been to show up at his house this morning, but the fall put me out of commission. I'd prefer to see him when I'm not writhing in pain."

It would be counterproductive to ask him why he hadn't phoned someone else then. Unless he didn't have a phone, but she didn't believe it. The problem between him and his father was more grave than she'd supposed. "I've been given a car to use and will fill your prescription if you'll tell me where to get it."

"I have to pick it up in person."

"Since you're in no shape to get behind a wheel, I'll drive you." She saw the cane on the table and handed it to him. "After you."

She followed him out, locking the door behind her, then she ran ahead of him and opened the back door of the car. When he'd climbed in with difficulty and more or less lay against the seat, she shut his door and got in the driver's seat.

"Are you hiding, or is that position more comfortable?"

"Both. Follow the road to Salerno." His words sounded like they came through gritted teeth. "There's a *farmacia* in the Piazza Municipio seven miles from here that will be open."

When she'd found the main road she said, "What would you have done if I hadn't come when I did?"

"I was on the verge of calling for a taxi when I heard the car in the drive." He sat up, obviously not worried about being recognized now that they were on the road. Annabelle heeded his precise instructions to get them to the other town. Traffic was heavy. She knew he was suffering, but he'd chosen to be stubborn by hiding out in his own house unannounced and she refused to feel sorry for him.

What was it Guilio had said about her being stubborn like his son? It had frustrated him when she'd told him she refused to intrude on him and his wife while she was in Ravello.

Eventually she slowed to a stop in front of the store. "We've arrived." There were no drive-thru pharmacies here.

"Don't move from this spot. With luck I won't run in to anyone I know."

Maybe not, she mused, but he'd certainly be noticed. Lucca's tall male physique would do wonders for anything he wore including the tan chinos and raspberry-colored polo shirt she hadn't noticed until now. In uniform, he'd really be something.

Knowing he was about to get the relief he craved, she noticed he managed to move quickly with that cane. While she waited for him, her cell phone rang. When she saw Cavezzali on the ID, guilt swamped her. If she didn't answer, he might get worried.

She clicked on. "Hello? Guilio? How are you?"

"*Molto bene*, Annabelle. Basilio told me Giovanni is ecstatic about the pictures he took today."

Thank goodness. "That's wonderful."

"I will come to Amalfi tomorrow. I have some new ideas for the shoot."

"I'll look forward to seeing you."

"Are you comfortable at the farmhouse? Do you need anything?"

Now was the time to tell him. "The farmhouse is a dream, but I've discovered modeling makes me tired and I don't want to do any cooking. So I've made arrangements to stay at the Casa Claudia for the rest of my time here. There are the most fabulous food places all around it."

"That's a good little family establishment. I was afraid the farmhouse might be too isolated."

"You were right after all. I'm sorry you went to that trouble for me. Please don't send any maids. I've cleaned everything including the fridge and will give you back the key later."

"I'm glad you changed your mind."

Only because of Lucca's entry into her life. She'd loved being by herself at the farm, where she could do exactly as she pleased, but a certain unexpected event had changed the situation.

"In truth, I love all the little places to eat. Italian cuisine is the best! I could eat my head off here, but I know I've got to be careful or I won't be able to fit in to the clothes Marcella has chosen for me."

In the midst of Guilio's laughter, Lucca got back in the car. She decided to put the phone on speaker. The last thing she wanted was for him to think she was talking behind his back with his father. Maybe hearing his father's voice would influence Lucca to contact him.

"I'm not worried, Annabelle. Don't forget the party I'm giving a week from Saturday. You'll be meeting our top Italian dealers. I've decided to give everyone a preview to whet their appetites before the big launch." The excitement in his voice was palpable. She was ready to disconnect them if he started to say anything that would give away the surprise.

"I know how much this means to you." So far the man in the backseat had no idea this was all in tribute to him. "I'll give you my very best."

"You always do. Did I tell you Mel Jardine will be coming next week? He's missing you terribly."

"I miss him, too," she said, warmed by his words, "but I have to admit I love it here."

"That's what I like to hear. Does that mean you're reconsidering my offer?" he asked hopefully.

"No. It just means I'm a typical woman who's having more fun than I deserve."

"After what you've been through, no one deserves it

more than you. Now get to bed and I'll see you tomorrow."

"Thank you for everything, Guilio. *Ciao.*"

Once Annabelle had clicked off, she turned in the
seat and was taken back by Lucca's inscrutable stare.
The light from the store illuminated his irises, which
were flecked with green among the grey. What a beautiful surprise they were. This was the first time she'd
seen their color.

The silence deepened, making her uneasy. "Are you
waiting for your prescription to be filled?"

"No. I've taken my medicine and am ready to go
home whenever you are."

The knowledge that he would be feeling relief shortly
seemed to have revived him enough to be civil to her.
He might hate it that she existed as an unwanted encum-
brance, but he'd needed someone to help him. Would
it be out of the question to hope he might thank her at
some point? She started the car and headed back to
Ravello without saying anything.

"My father sounded more excited than I've heard
him in years."

*You have no idea, Lucca.* "After meeting him, I had
the impression he's always like that."

"You've heard of the immovable object and the ir-
resistible force. My father's the embodiment of both of
them," he said in a tone of exasperation.

Her thoughts flew to Guilio, who came across as a
dynamo and was infinitely likable. But she hadn't been
his child who'd lived with him from birth. That child
might have a different perspective altogether.

About to ask him if he needed anything else as long
as they were out, she decided against it because it was

quiet back there. Annabelle would normally be turned off by such moody behavior, but she knew too much about him already and cared about him in spite of herself. The man had served his country and was used to making instantaneous decisions to take out the enemy and still stay alive.

That kind of sacrifice put him in a special category of human being, particularly since he'd suffered a recent leg injury that had brought him home on unexpected leave. She imagined it wasn't in his nature to show his need of anyone. Proud to a fault, perhaps? Especially around his father? It had to be a man thing.

Being a survivor, he would shun anyone hovering over him. Annabelle could understand that and wished she hadn't been in his house last night. The wounded warrior had the right to come home and deal with his demons out of sight.

It was a case of her being in the wrong place at the wrong time. Guilio couldn't have known that. He'd only been trying to accommodate her.

A shudder wracked her body when she thought of the cruel things she'd said to Lucca. Once she'd realized who he was and had overcome her fear, anger hadn't been far behind. She knew most—if not all—of her comments last night had more to do with lashing out at Ryan. He often came home in the middle of the night after being on rounds at the hospital. Or so she'd thought.

Instead he'd been with the woman who was now his wife. They had a baby, the one that should have been Annabelle's. The one Ryan had said they couldn't have until he'd become a fully fledged doctor and had set up a practice.

No...those salvos she'd enjoyed hurling last night had been aimed at the wrong target. If Lucca ever gave her a chance to explain, she would apologize.

By the time they reached the house, she thought he must have fallen asleep. In fact she was sure of it when she opened the rear door and called to him several times without obtaining a response. The position he was half lying in couldn't possibly have been comfortable. If it were, she'd let him spend the night there.

She reached for the cane and propped it against the side of the car. "Lucca?" She nudged his shoulder gently. "Wake up! You're home now. Let me help you in the house. Come on. You can't stay here."

Something she'd said, maybe just the sound of her voice, must have gotten through to him. Suddenly his body turned rigid and jerked upright. Streams of words poured from his mouth in rapid succession. They hadn't been said in anger or swearing. Though she understood very little Italian, she thought he must be giving orders or delivering instructions.

In the semidark, a look of horror spread across his face. The hand closest to her squeezed her upper arm in a death grip. He was unaware of his strength. His cries rang in the night air. She thought he said a name before low sobs of anguish shook his frame and found their way to her soul.

Whatever he was reliving in his mind had to have been unspeakable. The man battled post-traumatic stress disorder. Annabelle had worked around vets at the hospital and understood even more his natural instinct to hide away from family until he was able to cope.

Still standing, she leaned farther in and put her other

arm around his shoulders. Without conscious thought she rocked him against her, pained for him. "You're all right, Lucca. It's just a dream. You're home and safe," she murmured over and over in soothing tones, wanting to comfort him.

The freshly shaven male cheek pressed against hers was damp with tears. Whether his or hers at this juncture, she didn't know. "It's all right," she whispered against his temple. "I'm with you. Wake up," she cried softly.

After a long moment his hold on her arm loosened enough for her to embrace him fully. In the next breath she felt his body relax, as if he were with her now, mentally as well as physically. No longer seized by what had to have been some kind of flashback, he drew in a labored breath.

His hands roamed her waist and back experimentally. She felt their warmth before they moved around to slide up her arms and cup her face. He gazed at her, still disoriented.

"Hi," she whispered, struggling to keep a steady voice while her body was still reacting to his touch. "Remember me?"

After a silence he said, "*Signorina* Marsh."

"Yes. You had a bad dream on the way home from the pharmacy, but it's over now."

Their lips were close enough she could feel his breath on them. "Did I have one last night?" The man was suffering. Her heart went out to him.

"To be honest, I don't know. As soon as you fell asleep, I moved to the other bedroom. Tell me what happened to you in the war, Lucca. Talk to me! I take it your jet crashed."

Suddenly his hands gripped her upper arms. Even in the semidark, his face darkened. "How much did you hear?"

"Enough to understand what's bottled up inside you."

"You really want to know?" he muttered fiercely.

"Yes! I don't care how terrible."

His fingers tightened, but she knew he had no idea of his strength. "Our squadron was under enemy fire." She heard his labored breathing. "I watched my best friend get blown out of the sky. Why did it have to be him and not me?" His anguish devastated her. "He had a wife and a baby on the way. I couldn't understand why I was alive and he wasn't."

She rubbed his cheek. "After any kind of disaster, the person who survives always feels guilt. It's a normal human reaction. In time, it'll go away. I promise."

"I want to believe you."

"Tell me what happened after that."

"My jet took a hit." The cords in his neck stood out. "I ejected before the next round of fire finished it off. When I came to, I realized I'd ended up a junk heap on a pile of rocks. It took three days before a helicopter found me in that war zone and flew me out of there."

"It must have felt like three years." His pain had to have been excruciating.

"I drifted in and out of consciousness." But she heard the pain in his voice. "After I was picked up, I was transported to a field hospital for immediate treatment. From there I was flown to Germany."

"How long were you in the hospital?"

"Once I was transported there, four months. My thigh bone was broken across the shaft. They had to insert a metal plate."

Annabelle swallowed hard. "That was a bad break, but you didn't lose your leg, thank heaven." She sounded breathless even to her own ears. "The screw-and-plate treatment does help you heal faster."

She heard his sharp intake of breath. "Provided you don't try to climb a steep hill and then crash on the tiles in the dead of night."

Without conscious thought she rested her forehead against his. "What else can you expect from a crack Italian jet pilot so used to protecting others, he forgot about his own safety."

An odd sound came from his throat. He smoothed his thumbs over her moist skin. "I'm not fit to be around, but you seem to have survived listening to me. That was your first mistake." Once more he was on the defensive. "Now you're stuck with me for a while longer."

He'd just given her the answer to the question plaguing her earlier. He hadn't contacted his father yet.

As he removed his palms from her cheeks, she backed away so he could get out of the car. "I believe this is yours." She gave him the cane.

After he emerged, she shut the door. With the feel of his hands still on her making her feel all trembly, she hurried ahead and opened the door to the kitchen. Once they were both inside, she locked it before turning on the light. He moved to the sink and took another drink from the tap, then turned to her.

The latest dose of medication taken in the pharmacy had removed some of the grimace lines. His eyes reflected more green than grey at the moment. Like his father, he had a strong nose and chin. Lucca's features had a more chiseled cast.

She was struck by the warmth of his olive complexion,

the vibrant black of medium-cropped hair and winged brows. Without pain tightening his lips, the mouth that had come close to touching hers moments ago appeared wider than she'd realized. Sensuous even. He was a gorgeous-looking male specimen uniquely Italian, but that wasn't the important thing here.

"When you're ready to go to bed, call me."

"I thought you were going to pack and leave."

"I'll do it tomorrow after work. But any vet leaving the hospital having PTSD should have someone nearby. At least for tonight."

Her comment appeared to have taken him back. "So you're willing to put yourself in jeopardy a second time?"

"Like you said last night, you couldn't if you wanted to, and you don't want to. Did I get that right?"

"*Perfetto.*" Were those little green sparks shooting from the slits of his eyes?

"Good. Then we understand each other. After you get into a comfortable position, I'll put pillows between your legs to relieve the strain. You should feel less pain by morning. Maybe then you'll tell me when you plan to let your father know you're home."

"I'll tell you now." He cocked his head. "If I hadn't fallen, I would have called him this morning to come to the farmhouse so we could talk. But I was in too much pain. I wanted to be in the best shape possible when I told him my plans for the future, knowing he won't like them."

"Why? What *are* your plans?" Annabelle was dying to know.

"I think I was born wanting to farm, but by the time

I turned eighteen, my father wouldn't hear of it. He said a Cavezzali wasn't meant to farm."

Annabelle listened as he told her all the things his father had said to shut him down. It was a side of Guilio's nature she wouldn't have known about unless Lucca had decided to confide in her.

"My mother's family made their living that way and they were the happiest people you ever saw." His eyes lit up. "I liked learning how to grow things and watch the fruit trees change in different seasons. I learned everything from my mother and grandparents. When Papa set off for work, I went off early with Mama before school. We either did pruning, or we picked fruit. Whatever needed doing."

Lucca sounded so happy just talking about it, that happiness infected her. "I have no doubts it would be a wonderful life," she murmured.

"I doubt my father's opinion has changed over the years, but it's the life I want and he'll have to get used to it. If I'm feeling fit enough tomorrow, I'll phone him."

She nodded. "I'll be back in a minute with those pillows."

# CHAPTER THREE

Lucca found it easy to talk to Annabelle, but he realized he *was* wiped out. She'd been right about the PTSD and several other things. Before help had arrived, he'd been fighting pain and felt utterly drained. Though he'd lain around most of the day needing relief from the jabbing pain and finding none, bed had never sounded better.

Ten minutes later he'd brushed his teeth and had pulled on grey sweats and a white T-shirt. If he were alone in the house, he wouldn't have bothered with clothes. No sooner had the thought entered his mind than she appeared in the same robe she'd worn last night, holding two pillows and a glass of water. She'd fastened her hair at the nape.

"How did you know I was ready for you to come in?"

"I didn't. I'm working on *my* time schedule. When you didn't call out, I came anyway."

"Then—"

"Then I could have caught seeing you in the altogether," she said, coming around to the right side of the bed. She put the glass next to his bottle of pills. Something about her smelled like fresh lemons.

"I hate to tell you this, but I haven't been living for it. I'm afraid you don't want to know how many men—thin, fat, old, young and in between—I've helped change out of their inadequate hospital gowns, let alone shower. It wouldn't be a new sight, except for the face, of course," she said with a smile.

Lucca couldn't help chuckling. It had been ages since he'd done that.

"He laughs, ladies and gentlemen—and his face didn't crack," she teased. "Okay. Find your favorite way to sleep, then I'll fix you up."

Without thinking about it, he turned on his right side and carefully crossed his left leg over. His body felt like a dead weight. When he was settled, she fit the two pillows in between them. "This helps distribute the weight of your top leg over the whole length. That way there's less strain on the injured bone."

Lucca exhaled a heavy sigh. "Unfortunately when I'm asleep, who knows what I'll do."

"Who knows?" She flashed him a mysterious smile. "You might find your quilt on the floor in the morning. Or, you might actually enjoy a sound sleep in this position for a change." She put the covers over him before turning out the light, cloaking them in semidarkness, due to the moon.

When she left the bedroom, he felt an odd twinge of disappointment. Though she gave as good as she got under fire, she was one of the least unobtrusive women he'd ever met.

If his father didn't require nursing services, then what kind of job in advertising was she doing for him? He had to admit that when he'd heard the two of them talking on the phone earlier, his father hadn't sounded loverlike with her. His tone conveyed that he treated her more like a cherished friend.

What was the other offer Guilio had referred to on the phone, the one she'd turned down so blithely?

Lucca decided that whatever reason she had for not giving him away to Guilio, it couldn't be because she'd decided to come on to his son. That wasn't the kind of embrace she'd given Lucca. Hers had been full of compassion, the furthest thing from a plan of seduction. He'd been moved by it.

Over the years he'd enjoyed his share of women and knew the difference. But something else *was* motivating her.

There were many parts to *Signorina* Marsh still hidden. *Secrets.* While he lay there drifting in and out of sleep, he found himself wanting to expose them. His thoughts wandered all over the place until morning, when once again sunlight streamed through the window. The angle told him it was probably eight-thirty, nine o'clock.

He blinked. During the night he'd turned on his other side. Though his covers lay at the bottom of the bed and one pillow had fallen to the floor, the other one was still in place between his thighs.

Two things surprised him. His first instinct hadn't been to reach for his pills. The pillow trick must have worked because he hadn't awakened in pain. In fact it had subsided enough to give him a good night's sleep. The pills he'd taken last night were still working. He got to his feet actually feeling rested for a change. This morning he would make *café au lait* with sugar, the second best thing to *cappuccino.*

After freshening up in the bathroom, he wandered into the kitchen. Not until he reached it did he realize he hadn't grabbed for the cane lying on the bedside table.

His gaze darted to the terrace. *Signorina* Marsh, still in her robe, had placed one of the patio chairs near the railing. She sat there gazing over the view deep in thought while she sipped her coffee. He quickly heated up milk and fixed his own concoction before walking out to stand next to her.

She must have felt his presence and lifted her eyes. They were more blue than violet this morning. What woman could look so good without makeup? Her hair, caught loosely at the back of her head, hadn't been touched since last night. She was in bare feet.

"I don't need to ask how you slept," she murmured. "It's there on your face. I'm glad."

"Thanks to your expertise." He took a long swallow of his hot drink.

"It's good to see you feeling better, *signore*."

"You called me Lucca when you woke me out of my nightmare last evening. Since we've already slept together, let's drop the formality, shall we?" He watched heat spiral into her cheeks as he'd intended.

Their first night together had been an interesting one since he'd fallen asleep almost immediately. Looking at her right now, he found that incredible. What in the hell had been wrong with her husband?

She nodded. "I've been hoping you'd say that. Why don't you pull up the other chair and tell me what else is going on inside you."

In an instant his good mood vanished. "What are you? A psychiatrist now?"

"Maybe you need one."

"The hell I do—" Her mild-toned comment had pressed his hot button.

She didn't flinch. "During your nightmare you were

in combat mode and called out a name in agony. Last night you opened up to me, but you've only scratched the surface. Now that you're awake, you need to keep on talking."

"No thanks."

In an unexpected move, she got to her feet. "One of the doctors I trained under at the vet hospital explained that a man who has seen combat needs to validate his existence to another warm body. It's vital that what he did in the war did matter to at least one other human being besides himself.

"If you don't choose to use me for a sounding board, don't wait too long to find someone, Lucca. For your sake it's vital you pick out a person who wants to listen, and do it soon, even if it's a therapist. Is it that impossible to consider talking to your father?"

He darted her a piercing gaze. "You really do go where angels fear to tread."

"If our positions were reversed, wouldn't you want to help me?"

She had him there. During his time in the hospital, part of his therapy had been with a psychiatrist who'd told him everyone's war experience was a singular one. Those in combat lived, died or survived, yet humanity was scarcely aware of it. The worst thing he could do was remain mute.

Lucca closed his eyes and threw his head back. "How's this for starters? My father forbade me to go to the military academy in Bari. I went anyway against his wishes because I wanted to be like my grandfather, who'd fought in the previous war."

A stillness came over her. "I had no idea. Guilio never told me."

"No. He wouldn't. That's because his father-in-law came home minus his lower leg. It's not something my father likes to think about."

"The cane..." she cried softly "Was it his?"

"Yes. If you think my father wants to hear about my injury and relive that horror, then you're very much mistaken. But I realize he has to be told. Despite what I've been through and am still going through, you're not a man and don't understand how much I want to look substantial to him when he first sees me. Is that honest enough for you?"

Her eyes glazed over as she nodded. "I'm so sorry, Lucca," she whispered.

It had been a long time since anyone had responded that way out of concern for him. *It's been too long since you allowed anyone to see into that part of your soul, Cavezzali.* Her reaction surprised and touched him, stirring feelings inside him he hadn't had any idea were there.

"So am I."

"I feel very honored you would share that much with me. Maybe later you'll share more."

"There *is* no more."

"Oh, yes there is." Before he could countenance it, she raised up on tiptoe and pressed a brief kiss to his cheek. Then she quietly moved the chair over to the table and walked back in the house with her empty cup.

He stood at the railing for a long time, realizing he needed to call the doctor. The hospital had arranged for him to see one in Solerno for a checkup and more medication.

Maybe fifteen minutes passed before he heard her car pull out of the driveway. A new sense of emptiness stole through him. He disliked the fact that she was the cause of it. Why *this* woman? *She's getting to you, Cavezzali.*

*Diavolo!*

*You fool, Annabelle.*

As he'd said, this morning she'd had to go to a place even the *angels* knew to avoid! Now she'd forced Lucca to open up in ways he might resent her for later. Oh she hoped not! But even if he did, this had been a major step for him to start the healing process.

How would Guilio respond when Lucca faced him? His son's injury would pain him. The fact that Lucca hadn't told him he was back yet would pain him. She knew that. It pained *her*. She was in pain for Lucca.

He hadn't told her everything. The vision of what he'd held back sent a shudder through her body because she'd seen and heard part of it already during his flash-back. She marveled that he'd survived and she was absolutely in awe of his instinct for self-preservation.

That was the problem. At this point she felt an affection for *both* men that ran deep. She wanted to help, but it wasn't her place.

She would love to blame this whole situation on Guilio. He'd related so many happy memories of his first wife and their endearing, handsome son, she'd been curious about Lucca long before meeting him.

Her guilt deepened because she hadn't told him the exact nature of her work for his father. He was too intelligent a man not to know she'd been less than forth-coming. Yet unlike her, he hadn't forced the situation out in the open yet, but it was probably only a matter of time.

Fortunately she had a new place to stay and would move there after work. If she ever got there... The traffic in Amalfi was horrendous. She needed all her powers of concentration.

Thanks to the map and specific directions Guilio had provided after settling her at the farmhouse, she found the Hotel Europa overlooking the Piazza Sant'Andrea. Their parking garage had never been more welcome. If her employer hadn't set everything up ahead of time for this special photo shoot, it couldn't have happened, not here in this crowded tourist mecca.

"Ah, you've arrived—" Guilio met her in the foyer and swept her up the stairs to a suite on the next floor.

"I'm not late, am I?"

"No, but Marcella needs more time."

"Why?"

"When I saw the proofs taken in Rome, I was so elated with the outcome, I decided we would substitute a wedding dress for the businesswoman's suit layout planned for today's shoot. She brought several of her own bridal creations. We need to see you in all of them before a final decision is made."

Annabelle didn't mind trying on the various signature outfits meant for someone else. Her own wedding was past history. She'd been there and done that, except her bride's dress hadn't been a gown like one of these $50,000 selections.

The whole crew gathered round to give input. Each rendition was breathtaking in its own way. "Ah," they all cried when she donned the last one of filmy silk and lace.

"That's it!" Guilio declared, voicing his approval above the others.

Giovanni squinted at her before turning to the hairdresser. "Let her hair flow like a maiden's. It will make the most of the mantilla. I'll arrange it after we're outside."

With those words everyone went to work on her. Marcella told one of the assistants to carry the matching high heels out to the piazza, where Annabelle would put them on. For the final touch she wore a dazzling diamond choker and matching diamond earrings. When all was ready and her makeup perfect, she left the room in her sandals and they went down the stairs with the assistants, who carried the long lace train.

People in the packed hotel foyer started clapping. It grew louder as she moved out the doors into the piazza, where she was met with more oohs and aahs. Police had cordoned off the area where a gleaming, flame-red Amalfi convertible sports car stood parked at the base of the ancient staircase. The famed fourteenth century cathedral of Saint Andrew awaited at the top.

Guilio must have seen her expression. "We won't ask you to climb all sixty-two steps."

She laughed to cover her gulp.

Once Giovanni had arranged the floor-length lace mantilla to his liking and she'd stepped into the high heels, he announced he was ready. Leaning close he whispered, "When his son sees this picture, he'll run off with the *bellissima* Amalfi Girl. Every woman on the coast will mourn the loss of the sought-after Cavezzali bachelor."

Her heart raced for no reason. "Right." But she covered her sarcasm with a wink.

Annabelle had news for the photographer. Lucca had already seen her in the flesh. The last thing he wanted to do was run off with the woman who was an intruder in his home. Giovanni, artistic to his core, didn't have a clue about the pilot who'd come back from the war agonizing physically and emotionally.

But the photographer's comment, meant to flatter her, only hit her harder for keeping quiet about Lucca in front of Guilio. As heat poured guilty color up her neck into her face, Marcella unwittingly saved her from having to talk by handing her flowers. Annabelle lifted the bridal bouquet and inhaled the fragrance of the white stephanotis interspersed with tiny flame-red tea roses.

"We want you to try several poses." Basilio took over. He opened the passenger door, revealing the ultraposh tan leather interior, where a long-stemmed rose of flame-red lay on the seat. "First, walk up the steps until your whole train is exposed. Look back toward the car as if waiting for your bridegroom."

Thanks to Giovanni's comment, an image of Lucca rather than Ryan passed through her mind. In a tuxedo, he'd be spectacular. When she realized where her thoughts had wandered, she took a sharp breath and tried harder to follow instructions.

A few more touches here and there and the shoot began. Basilio wanted different looks. So did Guilio. Between the two men, who got into animated conversations and gesticulated with their hands, the day wore on and on. Giovanni had endless energy and continued in his upbeat way to encourage her, but finally even he declared they had enough film.

Relieved it was over, Annabelle hurried inside the hotel. After being dejeweled and disrobed, she freshened up. Once she'd removed her makeup, she changed into her sleeveless orange linen shirtwaist and sandals.

Guilio was waiting for her and invited her to eat dinner with him and his wife at their villa.

Not wanting to offend him, she asked if she could take a rain check because she was nursing a slight headache. It wasn't far from the truth. "This modeling business is much harder than I thought."

He patted her arm. "The sun was warm today. By all means go back to the hotel and have an early night."

"That and a cold drink are all I need, Guilio." Once she knew if Lucca was all right, she'd be able to relax. "Thanks for understanding. Will you be at the shoot tomorrow in Furore?"

"No. I have to fly to Milan for an important meeting, but I'll be back the day after. You can always call me if anything comes up."

"I know. Thank you."

"I told Marcella to save that wedding dress for you with my compliments."

"Guilio—you're generous to a fault, but there's no wedding in my future. I'm done." He knew she was divorced though she'd never told him the details.

A frown appeared. "Only the young say that without knowing what's around the next corner."

"I think you're mixing me up with the Amalfi Girl who still has stars in her eyes. She hasn't been where I've been and doesn't know those stars blaze hot, then run out of hydrogen and fade." From the doorway she blew him a kiss, then hurried down to the parking garage.

The evening traffic was even worse than the morning commute. By the time she pulled in the driveway, her worry over an untenable situation combined with fatigue had caused her temples to throb.

After parking the car, she hurried inside, moving past Lucca, who was cooking something at the stove. The duffel bag was nowhere in sight. A delicious aroma filled the house, even to the bathroom.

Annabelle had to admit she was glad their earlier conversation hadn't driven him away or put him off his food. On the way home from Amalfi, her anxiety level had gone off the charts. She'd feared she might find him in a more troubled state than the night he'd come home.

She reached for the bottle of ibuprofen she'd put in the cabinet. Two pills ought to do it. Cupping her hands, she trapped the water from the faucet and swallowed. In the process, her hair fell forward and some of it got wet. She reached in her purse for the tortoiseshell clip she carried and fastened the ends behind her head.

When she walked back to the kitchen, she couldn't help but notice how good he looked in another black shirt, a polo this time, and jeans. When she'd asked Marcella what it was about Italian men and their clothes, she said it was because the Italian mother considered her son to be so important, she pushed him to turn out gorgeous no matter what. She would actually starve herself to save the money to keep him stylish.

Annabelle smiled, not knowing if that was totally true, but in Italy she'd been surrounded by men who dressed with uncommon flare. Lucca was no exception. Even in the sweats and T-shirt he'd worn to bed last night, he'd looked classy, yet he seemed unconscious of it.

"Something smells delicious."

He was pouring a white sauce over the baked pasta

in a tomato base that was arranged in a large oval dish. "It does to me, too. I've made my favorite meal."

"What is it?"

"Veal cannelloni."

"Did your mama teach you?" Her mind was still on her conversation with Marcella.

"She taught me many things." The affection in his voice was palpable. He'd been his mama's boy all right. Italian men were known for putting their mothers on a pedestal. "Are you hungry?"

The change in his spirits from this morning came as a big shock. "Yes." All of a sudden she was famished.

"Then join me on the terrace and help me eat this."

He was feeling better and wanted to show her. She couldn't turn him down. "Would you like me t—"

"No," he interrupted. "I've managed pretty well on my own today."

He certainly had. "I can see that." So would his father when the time came.

Something dramatic had caused this alteration in his mood. She knew that getting him to open up was partially responsible.

While he carried the hot dish outside, she followed and sat down in one of the chairs. A lighted candle flickered over the table already set for two. On top of the floral cloth he'd placed bread and salad. Between the scent of flowers in the air and the wonderful smell of the cannelloni, it was all too romantic for words.

She watched him sit. He was still careful, but she was confident his pain was diminishing. He served her a sample of everything. "I made tea with lemons from the fruit on that overhang, but if you'd prefer wine, there's some in the cupboard. I won't be drinking any until I'm off my painkillers."

"Tea sounds perfect to me. What a good patient you are!"

"Actually I was the hospital's worst," he corrected her after starting in on his food. "By the time the doctors told me I'd healed enough to leave, they were ready to throw me out, but my psychiatrist said I wasn't ready. He was right. So were *you*."

Annabelle almost choked on the bread she was in the middle of swallowing. "About this morning—"

"We both know I have post-traumatic stress," he blurted before she could finish her thought. "The doctor told me I don't suffer from it as badly as some of the other guys he's treated, but I've been living in denial that it was my problem. You dashed water in my face and woke me up. It's what I needed, so don't apologize."

"If this meal is your way of thanking me, then I'm very humbled." She wiped the corner of her mouth with the napkin. "Thank you for not staying angry with me." The man had a lethal charm she couldn't deny.

"Since it serves both our purposes to live under the same roof, I decided we might as well enjoy our partnership in crime together."

"Lucca...you can't tease about something this serious. After we eat, I really am going to leave. I've already registered at the Casa Claudia."

His facial muscles tautened. "Why would you do that? This morning you offered me your services. Did I misunderstand?"

"No. That offer is still open, but not here in your home. Whether you realize it or not, I care for your father and can't bear the guilt I feel still pretending I don't know you're back in Ravello." She bit her lip. "Yes, I'm worried about my standing in his eyes, but aren't you afraid he'll somehow find out? He loves you. What if it's too much of a shock for him?"

Any parent would be hurt, especially Guilio, with all his plans. She dreaded what his reaction would be to know his son had been staying at the farmhouse with Annabelle and she'd said nothing.

His eyes narrowed on her features. "I'll call him tomorrow and explain everything. I swear it."

Annabelle believed him. "You have no idea how relieved I am to hear it."

"He'll understand I placed you in a terrible position and won't give it another thought. But since we're discussing your sins of omission, how about the one against me."

She was ready to tell him the truth. "Your father met me in California while he was over there on business. He came right out and asked me if I would fly to Italy for three weeks to be a model in a new campaign ad he was working on."

Lucca blinked. "You're a model?"

"Don't flatter me too much," she teased after hearing the surprise in his question.

"You know very well you're easy on the eyes," he drawled. "Go on. This conversation is getting more fascinating by the second."

"I told you I'm a nurse, but he said I had the look he wanted."

"He's never used a female model before."

"I found that out. The other day on one of the shoots I asked him again, 'Why me?' He said I have that all American look and smile that appeals to men who buy his cars. Apparently he's made a study of it or something."

Laughter escaped his throat, surprising her because she so rarely heard it from him and because he was so attractive when he did laugh.

"What's so funny?"

"My father. He's good. In fact he's so good at what he does, even I stand in awe of him. What he really means in the American vernacular is that you're drop-dead gorgeous to every male in sight."

"I think you must be your father's son. You're good at what you do, too. No one's ever told me that before. You've made my heart pound out of rhythm."

When she realized she was actually flirting with him, she couldn't believe it. Not after the winter she'd been living in since the divorce.

He lounged back in the chair. "Where were you when I was recuperating in hospital?"

"Probably changing some old man's dressing at another hospital. Back then who would have dreamed that one day you'd be relaxing on your own terrace, let alone feeding your home-crasher divine cannelloni you learned to make at your mother's feet?"

He angled his dark head toward her. "You liked it?"

"Trust me, you could open up your own restaurant on your farming property."

"Now there's an idea! In that case I'll come up with something else to satisfy your taste buds for tomorrow night's menu."

*Tomorrow night.* The thought of it filled her with a fluttery sensation. "You mean you're going to feed me in return for my listening to you."

Lucca examined her with a speculative glance. "It

makes perfect sense to me. By the way, I need some things from the store. How would you like to drive me to the *farmacia* in Solerno for more shaving cream and blades. Unless you're too tired."

"Not at all." She'd taken something for her headache earlier, but it was the transformation in Lucca that had given her a second wind. She was pleased he was feeling this much better.

What alarmed her was how thrilled she was to be able to spend more time with him this evening. This shouldn't be happening. "We'd better hurry before it closes. I'll get my purse. After we get back, I'll do the dishes."

He got to his feet. "There's a rule in this house. Whoever does the cooking, does the cleaning up." He blew out the candle and followed her inside.

A half hour later they'd made the trip and she came out of the *farmacia* with the desired toiletries. When she would have gotten back in the car he said, "You see that *trattoria* across the piazza?"

"Yes?"

"It's been here for years. They serve a dessert to go called *torta caprese*. I think you'll like it."

"I could go for a *torta*," she said, mimicking his accent.

"*Bene*." When he smiled like that, she had difficulty catching her breath. "Use the money I gave you to buy some for us. I've decided you were right about something else you said earlier. I need a little sweetening up."

Following that thought she felt another dart of awareness at being alone with him like this. "I'll be right back."

Annabelle wouldn't have said anything else, not when he was coming out of that dark place where he'd been thrust months ago. His appetite was returning and he'd unburdened himself to an extent. It had to mean he was on the emotional mend, but she needed to be careful that she didn't read more into this than the situation warranted.

Lucca was Guilio's son, just home from war, and she'd happened to be on the premises to offer some support. But in less than two weeks she'd be going home. To construe any more out of this would be absurd. If she'd taken it slower with Ryan after they'd first met, she might have picked up on a clue and not have married him. She needed to remember that.

The errand didn't take her long. When she returned, Lucca told her where to drive. Five minutes later he'd guided them to a private place where the view of lights along the coastline filled her vision.

"If the whole world could see what I'm seeing," she murmured.

"Climb in back and we'll look together while we eat."

His suggestion made sense because he'd done enough standing and moving for one day. Yet she couldn't help feeling like she was a teenager getting in the backseat of a guy's car, ostensibly to watch an outdoor movie.

The trouble was, she took too long before she acted. When she joined him, he leaned closer and whispered, "I still couldn't if I wanted to, *Annabellissima*."

# CHAPTER FOUR

STEADY, Annabelle.

During the conversation with Marcella about the well-dressed Italian male, the designer had also given her tips about the Italian male himself. "They're born flirts. It's in their genes. They love women, all kinds, sizes and shapes.

"When they flatter you, they mean it, but don't assume it is a serious affair of the heart. A foreign woman does not understand this. She thinks she has his exclusive interest, which, of course, she does at the time, but it's not forever. He loves life, he loves love. The Italian woman understands this."

Annabelle decided Marcella gave out good advice. The change in Lucca from that first night in the hall was like night and day and had thrown her off her guard. As long as she knew to stay on guard, she'd be all right.

"I like your nickname for me, Lucca. No one else I've met has thought of it. It's very clever in fact, if you don't mind my saying." She felt him give her an odd glance while she pulled their cartons out of the sack and opened them. "Here you go. And a spoon."

"This is a local specialty," he informed her. "I've been salivating for one of these for ages."

"How long has it been since you were here last?"

"Maybe eight years."

"That's too long a time to be away from *this*." She'd almost said *home*, but caught herself in time.

He was too busy eating to comment.

"Umm," she moaned with pleasure after eating several mouthfuls. "It's like an undercooked brownie, but much better with that almond flavor. I can't stop with just one. I should have bought seconds."

He lounged back when he'd finished, looking amused. "When I stumbled up the hill between the fruit trees a few nights ago, I couldn't imagine being alive by morning. Now here I am stuffing myself with sweets in the backseat of a car with my new nurse."

No doubt he'd beguiled a ton of willing Italian female nurses, but he didn't know who he was dealing with. She put their empty cartons back in the sack. It was time for this American female nurse to go into action. He'd confided part of his soul to her. Now it was her turn so he wouldn't get the wrong idea that she was blindly attracted to him.

"I, too, can remember one night in the past believing that I wouldn't live through it."

She saw his expression quicken with curiosity.

"One of the nurses working on my shift at the hospital told me my husband had been having a full-blown affair with another nurse, whom I thought had been my friend."

Lucca eyed her for a lengthy moment. "When did it happen?"

"Two years ago. But evidently I did survive, and now here I am having eaten a decadent dessert with an Italian war hero. Who would have thought?" Before this went on any longer, she reached for the handle and got out of the car.

He continued to stare at her. "I hope you realize your ex-husband didn't deserve you. But if you're still so in love with him you can't sit still, then *you* need to talk about it."

She let out a measured breath. "My love for Ryan was burned out of me when I learned their relationship had been going almost from the beginning of our marriage."

After a period of quiet he asked, "How long were you married?"

"A year and a half." She stopped herself before she said anything more. Lucca didn't want to hear it, not when it sounded so trivial after what he'd lived through. She shut the door and opened the driver's door to get in.

"A very wise nurse I met the other night explained that a man who has seen combat needs to validate his existence to another warm body," Lucca continued as if she hadn't left the backseat. "It's vital that what he did in the war did matter to at least one other human being besides himself. *You've* been in combat of a different kind, Annabelle. Isn't that what my father meant about you deserving a break?"

She started up the car. "Yes."

"Why didn't you get help for it?"

*Touché.*

She waited until they were out on the main road before answering him. "I did. I divorced him and transferred to another hospital in Los Angeles."

"And now you're involved with this Mel Jardine?"

Lucca didn't miss much. "I met him after I moved to L.A."

"Where were you living before you moved?"

"In Fullerton. It's near L.A., where my family lives. My husband was finishing his residency at the same hospital where I'd been getting my nursing degree."

She heard him grind out something in Italian that needed no translation.

"You know what they say about a change being as good as a vacation, Lucca. At my lowest ebb, Mel offered me a job with his company. I took it and never looked back."

As she rounded a curve, another car started passing her. She had to brake so there wouldn't be an accident. That was all they would need, especially Lucca, whose surgery needed more time to really heal.

"Speaking of looking back, keep your head down. We're coming into Ravello. One of your family members or friends might be driving around and see you."

"In the backseat no less."

"And *alone*," she quipped. "No sign of lipstick on your mouth. Just chocolate." Giovanni wouldn't believe it.

A scoffing sound reached her ears and Annabelle grinned.

"So where do you go for these photo shoots?"

He was full of questions. "Besides Rome, where I've already been, they've been scheduled around the most beautiful spots along the Amalfi Coast. Basilio has been the one working with me the most, but your father's in charge of everything."

A brief silence prevailed before he asked her another question. "How did you meet my father exactly?"

"At Mel Jardine's dealership in L.A. He sells more Amalfis than any other in the States. Two months ago your father flew there to talk business with him."

Through the rearview mirror she saw Lucca's head lift. "You work for *that* dealership?"

"Yes."

"After being a nurse?" He sounded incredulous.

At last they were home safe and hopefully still undiscovered, but it didn't matter now that Lucca had promised to call his father. After she'd pulled in the drive, he climbed out of the back with the sacks. In the darkness he made an imposing figure. "What do you do for him. Don't tell me you sell cars."

"I won't. I'm Mel's private secretary."

"There *is* no such animal with the Cavezzali dealers." He stood there looking perplexed with his hands outstretched, Italian to the core. She wished she didn't find him so...appealing.

"That's true, but he created the job after his heart attack." She hurried ahead of him and let them in the house.

When she would have gone straight to the terrace to start cleaning up, he caught her hand. "Not yet. I want to hear the rest to the part where my father comes into this."

He wasn't about to let it go. Naturally he was curious. In fact he'd shown amazing restraint up to now. "I have to be to work early in the morning, but I'll make a deal with you. If you'll let me help you with the dishes, I'll tell you. We can get them done faster so you can get off that leg."

With seeming reluctance Lucca let her hand slip out

of his, but it left warmth curling up her arm to envelop her whole body. "The house doesn't have a dishwasher."

"It does now." She smiled at him. "I'll clear the table while you fill the sink."

He returned her smile. Another one without shadows. *Mama mia,* as they said back in old Napoli.

"You made quite a mess in the kitchen," Annabelle commented a few minutes later, "but it was worth it."

Lucca's arms were up to his elbows in suds. He scooped a few and blew them softly in her face. "Compliments won't get you out of telling me what I want to know."

She rinsed in the other sink and started wiping bowls and pans. "To make a long story short, Mel was one of my patients. He'd had a heart attack and needed special nursing after he left the hospital. The man is superenergetic and very persuasive. He arranged with my supervisor for me to go home with him for a few weeks."

He glanced at her. "I take it you wouldn't have consented unless you'd wanted to."

"No. He's very kind and treats me like a daughter really. Mel's a widower and his grown children don't live nearby. Though he has a housekeeper, he needed a nurse. We formed a friendship.

"When he got well enough to go back to work, the doctor cautioned him to cut down on his load and find an assistant to help handle his hectic schedule. Mel claimed I took such good care of him during his illness, he said he'd pay me triple what I made at the hospital if I'd come to work for him. So I did."

"From nursing to cars. Quite a jump from one arena to another that's vastly different."

"I know. My job description was to keep him sorted

out. I don't know about cars, but I can work with people."

"It's clear to me you'd be a natural at whatever you chose to do." She knew enough about Lucca to realize he never said what he didn't mean. His compliment meant more to her than it should have. She was starting to care too much. "What was the defining factor that made you accept his offer?"

She finished wiping the utensils and put them in the drawer. He'd been honest with her. Why not tell him the truth? What could it hurt?

"When I confronted my ex, he intimated our lives had been boring for a long time. Ryan wanted out of his mundane existence. He said that once we were married, the excitement went out of our relationship."

"Had you been intimate before the wedding?"

Annabelle had been in Italy long enough to notice that Italian men weren't afraid to talk about personal things. They got in your space. In that way they different from the American male.

She shook her head. Even if she'd thought the question audacious, they'd already gone way past desultory conversation to talk from those painful private places. "No. I was raised that you waited until you took your vows."

"So in order to win the prize, he had to marry you first."

"I never thought about it that way, but now that you mention it, I'm sure you're right."

"Some men are like that, Annabelle. Always needing another conquest to validate their existence. I've known rootless types like him."

"Rootless?"

"*Sì*," he said in his inimitable Italian way. "It's my theory they're not centered and therefore destined to be distracted by anything new that comes along, often discarding something or someone who's a pearl beyond price," he added in his deep voice.

A quiver ran through her body. Talking to Lucca was like inhaling a fresh, invigorating breeze. "I appreciate what you're saying, but I'm hardly a pearl. In all fairness, we both had periods where we did twenty-four-hour rounds, often at the wrong times. It wasn't a recipe for togetherness. There's a high ratio of divorce in that field. We ended up one of the statistics."

"You and half the world." She felt his intense gaze. "Your ex—Ryan, is it?—couldn't hold a candle to you."

His words were unexpected. The kind of words you wanted to hear when you weren't so sure of yourself anymore. Not even her husband had said things like that to her before they were married. "That's a lovely compliment, Lucca."

"It's only the truth."

She tossed her head back. "When I got married, I was so certain my marriage wouldn't fail. At the time of the divorce, Mel caught me at the moment when my pain was at its peak. In my vulnerability, I felt that some time away from medicine might be the best thing for me. I guess I thought it was time I stepped out of my predictable life and did something unpredictable. No reminders of the past.

"Mel and I already got along well. The transition to become his assistant didn't sound too difficult. Best of all, the kind of work I would do for him wouldn't tread on anyone else's toes. No one lost a job because of me. All those reasons fed into my decision, but in truth, I didn't want to be around the medical world, where the past would haunt me."

"That makes sense," he murmured. "Now we pan away to my father's arrival on the scene."

"Yes." Her pulse quickened. "The three of us spent several days together. He was gathering ideas for a new ad campaign and wanted my input from an American woman's perspective. I was amazed at his request, but it tickled me that he'd picked me over dozens of beautiful women who were professional models. As you can imagine, it was a boost to my sagging ego. Mel was willing to let me go if I promised to return by the end of June."

While she spoke, Lucca had been staring at her through veiled eyes, preventing her from knowing what he was thinking. "How much longer before you have to fly away?"

"Two weeks." Minus a day. She was dreading the day she had to go back and leave all this…leave Lucca. She carried the dishtowel and cloth to the utility area near the door of the kitchen and put it in the washer with some other things. After turning on the machine, she closed the door and turned to him. "In case you were wondering, Guilio did offer me a good sum of money to come, probably the going rate of a top model."

"I don't doubt it."

"I felt a fraud. What if the camera didn't like me? Out of that fear I told him I couldn't work for him unless I was paid the same salary Mel was paying me. After all, your father was virtually giving me a three-week holiday in Italy, all expenses paid plus the air fare over and back. To me that was a dream come true. In the end, he agreed."

He cocked his dark head. "My father is always in the driver's seat when it comes to establishing terms. For you to have the final say meant he wanted you here any way he could have you. So tell me—has it been a dream come true so far?"

She reeled from his question. Since Guilio had first approached her, she felt like she was in a dream, deathly afraid to wake up and find she was back in that dark place where she'd been existing. Annabelle couldn't bear the thought of ever being there again.

"So far it has been a thrill," she answered honestly, and Lucca was the major reason why. "Ask me again in two weeks. Good night." She started for the bedroom. He followed her down the hall.

"Don't go," he said in a husky tone. "I don't relish being left alone yet."

She turned to face him, alert to a nuance in his voice that sounded like he really meant it. "If you need to talk, just tell me."

"No. I'm too tired for that and know you must be, too." After a pause he said, "In a short period of time it seems I've got used to your company. I like the idea that you're just down the hall from me. You're easy to be around, do you know that? No woman of my acquaintance has ever had that particular quality."

"It's funny you'd say that. During the divorce Ryan accused me of having the opposite effect on him. He claimed he'd started walking on eggshells around me."

"But of course." His Italian shrug fascinated her. *Everything fascinated her.* "That was his guilt talking. In my country, there's a name for a man like that."

Something about the way he said that name caused her to smile. "In my country, too."

He reciprocated with a smile of his own. "As I was saying, you have a soothing effect that draws people to you. No wonder Mel Jardine didn't want to lose you after he left the hospital."

"Thank you," she whispered. This man knew to say all the right things. She was starting to get frightened by the strength of her feelings for him. "*Buona notte*, Lucca."

Lucca *had* got used to having her around. In just a few days he no longer felt like he was falling apart. He had Annabellissima to thank for this much of a sense of well being.

She was *bellissima*, from the inside out. Lucca wasn't about to let her go. He hadn't begun to plumb her depths.

It was time to talk to his father. Lucca decided to make good on his promise to her and call him now. Guilio would probably be in bed, but not asleep yet. Most likely he was enthralled in a good biography, his favorite kind of reading material.

After getting ready for bed, he stretched out in the most comfortable position for his leg and reached for the phone.

"*Lucca?*" his father cried after the second ring. From the sound of his voice, Lucca could tell he was wide-awake. That was good. "What a surprise to hear from you tonight! How are you, *figlio mio?*"

Much better than he'd expected to be when he'd first stumbled through the orchard to reach the farmhouse. "*Molto bene, Papa*. More to the point, how are you?"

"I couldn't be better now that I can hear your voice.

You're not still upset with me about not selling you those properties are you?"

Lucca gripped his phone tighter. "No matter how run-down they are, I still want to buy them, *Papa*, but that's not why I'm calling you now. I know it's late. If you want, I'll phone you back in the morning."

"Are you *demente*?" he boomed. "You call me, then you say I'll speak to you in the morning?"

His father would never change. "I just wanted to be sure you weren't too tired."

"If I were taking my last breath of life, I wouldn't be too tired to talk to you."

He felt his father's love and a bolt of guilt zapped him for not having called him sooner, but he hadn't gotten his pain under control until now. "I have a confession to make."

"What's another one in the long list of my son's antics?" his father teased.

"This is a big one."

"You got married and are bringing her home?" The hope in his father's voice never ceased to amaze him. To Guilio, marriage was everything. Certainly for his father, being married had kept his life stable and fulfilling.

"Not exactly. I've left the military for good."

After a pause Guilio said, "I don't believe it." His voice trembled for joy. "What will you do now that you're coming home?" he demanded.

"I'm going to be a farmer like I always wanted to be."

Rather than an outburst, for once all he heard was silence on the other end. Lucca knew it wasn't the answer his father was waiting to hear, but it had to be said. "*Papa*? Are you still there?"

"Of course I'm still here. There had to be a reason why you suddenly left the service. What was it?"

That brilliant business brain of his never stopped thinking. "I got an injury to my leg that makes me ineligible to be a pilot."

"How bad is it?" Guilio asked in a thick tone.

"I walked up the steep incline to the farmhouse on my own two legs. That's how bad I am." It was the truth. He was thankful to be able to say it.

"You mean you're in Ravello?" he bellowed.

"I was able to catch a military flight with some others guys and got here in the middle of the night. It was too late to disturb you and Maria. Unfortunately I fell by accident after letting myself in the farmhouse. So I loaded up on pain pills and have mostly slept. Would you believe I found an American woman named Annabelle sleeping in my bed?"

He'd managed to take his father's breath away. "You must have frightened her out of her skin!"

"Such beautiful skin, *Papa*. Actually she frightened the devil out of me when she started to call the police. I understand she's doing some modeling for a new ad campaign for you. To be honest, I can see why you picked her."

In spite of all the shocking news, his father managed to chuckle. "She's not as helpless as she looks."

"It's the nurse in her. When she found out I was your son and why I'd come home, she couldn't do enough to make me comfortable in my own home. I have to admit I like all the attention she's giving me. That's because she's crazy about you and upset that I took until tonight to call you. She's so loyal to you, I've been in the doghouse."

"That's gratifying to hear, but you have to understand something, Lucca. She's not like the other women who've come in and out of your life. This one is different."

"I know. As soon as she found out I'd come home, she registered at the Casa Claudia."

"You mean she has already moved out?"

"Not yet. She was planning to go in the morning, but I told her I hoped she would stay on. You know. Finders, keepers."

*"Lucca—"*

"Seriously, I like having her around and she loves this place. Since you installed her here first, I'd like her to stay. You can trust me to treat her like a princess."

"That's exactly what she is," his father grumbled. Shades of a lecture were in his voice. "Annabelle is a lady, just like your mother."

He blinked. Rare praise coming from his father. "I've already found that out, *Papa.* For one thing she wears her divorce like a shroud."

"She's been hurt."

"It's time she got over it. He didn't deserve her."

"Amen."

"Since the rooming arrangements have worked out for her so far, I've asked her to stay on, *Papa,* but that's up to her."

"If she's still with you, then it sounds like she's agreeable."

"I guess I'll find out tomorrow, but I'll be asleep most

of the day. The medication I'm on for pain puts me out for hours at a time. She makes sure I take it."

"It sounds like a nurse is exactly what you need. Under the circumstances I'm going to fly to Milan tomorrow and get some business out of the way." Lucca was surprised, but relieved, too, since it gave him another day to recuperate from his fall. "When I get back Monday morning, we'll spend the day together."

"Good. I want to buy those properties and settle down to work."

Again there was no outburst.

"*Papa,* remember that I'm not going anywhere."

More silence. "Do you have any idea how many years I've been waiting to hear those words?"

The lump in Lucca's throat grew a little larger. "Forgive me for waiting until I got home to call you?"

"What do you think?" he blurted in a voice gruff with emotion.

Tears smarted Lucca's eyes. "*Ti voglio bene, Papa.*"

"I love you, too. *Grazie a Dio* you're home in one piece."

Lucca seconded the motion. "The minute you're back in Ravello, come to the farmhouse. I'm going to make you a true Cavezzali breakfast."

"I'll be there, Lucca. In fact I'm already salivating."

"*Ciao,* Papa."

With his father's question about Annabelle going around in his head, he hung up and turned on the side he favored because of his leg to go to sleep. He had no doubts she wanted to stay. She *did* love the farm. What he'd told his father was the truth. It was very clear in the way she'd put flowers everywhere and sat dreamy eyed on the terrace breathing in the fragrance.

His last thought before he knew no more was that her fragrance was even more intoxicating.

Annabelle left the farmhouse before Lucca awakened and took off for her next destination. If he'd been up to say good-morning, she might have had difficulty leaving at all. Something was happening inside of her she didn't have the power to stop. Like a color enhancer on a movie cam, the world suddenly had a new brilliance.

She rounded the hairpin turn and fell instantly in love with the Amalfi convertible parked below the steeply terraced vineyards of Furore. The only way to describe the paint's color was to compare it to a semiprecious sea-green jade stone, light and lustrous. Combined with the creamy leather interior, it took her breath.

The crew hailed her. Basilio guided her to park behind the van as close to the wall of the road as possible. At this dizzying height, it was the only thing keeping all of them from falling into the sparkling blue depths below.

Being that it was a Saturday, everyone was anxious to get finished early and enjoy the rest of the weekend. The hairdresser quickly caught Annabelle's hair back in a loose chignon. Once her makeup was done, Marcella helped her into an eggshell-toned blouson of pin-tucked thin crepe.

The tucks ran vertically down the front, but were horizontal on the three-quarter sleeves. There was some chain-stitching detail Annabelle loved. The waist pulled it into shape over matching colored wide-legged pants.

After she'd put on sandals with bands of blue and green, Marcella produced a scarf the same color as the car's exterior and put it around her neck, knotting it loosely at the side. For an added touch, she put her in jade earrings.

The result brought a smile from Basilio, who proclaimed the whole effect perfection. Secretly Annabelle wished she could wear this outfit back to the farmhouse. She wanted to look beautiful for Lucca, but the price tag would be astronomical.

"What we want you to do is lean against the side of the car and reach for the bunch of purple grapes here. You saw these and you couldn't resist stopping for a taste. Giovanni will film you at various angles to capture the car as well as the view behind you."

"Be careful you don't drip juice if you bite into one," Marcella cautioned her.

Annabelle turned to Giovanni. "Do I have to eat them?"

"I don't know yet."

In the end he was satisfied with the shoot without her tasting the fruit. Both Annabelle and Marcella breathed a sigh of relief that the clothes weren't stained.

Basilio clapped his hands. "Everyone? We meet Monday morning in Sorrento. Eight o'clock sharp."

For a day and a half she was free. She went back to the van to change into her jeans and T-shirt. After removing all her makeup, she slipped into her car to go home and saw that it wasn't even one o'clock yet. She felt like a schoolgirl playing hooky for the rest of the day.

Lucca would be surprised to hear her drive in. He wouldn't be expecting her until evening. Would it be too much to ask that he'd already gotten in touch with his father to let him know he was back in Italy?

Until Guilio knew the truth, there was nothing to

work out with Lucca. Once Annabelle reached the farmhouse to freshen up, she would try to get her mind off
her worries and take off on a long drive. She would fill
her eyes with the mind-blowing scenery found only in
this part of the world. But when she pulled up in the
drive a little while later, thoughts of her day trip left
her mind when she saw another car parked there.

At first she thought it might be Guilio's. Or maybe it
was one of Lucca's stepbrothers on an errand of some
kind for their stepfather. But the car wasn't an Amalfi,
nor was it luxurious. Of course the visitor could be anyone, but it meant Lucca wasn't alone.

# CHAPTER FIVE

ANNABELLE got out of the car and entered the kitchen, not knowing what to expect. Voices drifted in from the living room. One belonged to a female. In between pauses, both were speaking Italian in hushed tones.

If Annabelle stayed in the kitchen, Lucca wouldn't know she was here. Since she didn't want him to discover her and think she'd been eavesdropping, she had no choice but to hurry down the hallway past the living room. That way he would see her on the way to her bedroom.

Out of the corner of her eye she glimpsed a dark-haired woman in his arms. She was probably Annabelle's age. Sobs punctuated her words. An old girlfriend perhaps? She had to be someone important to Lucca, a person he trusted implicitly, otherwise he wouldn't have told her she could come over.

The moment she closed her bedroom door, he rapped on it. "Annabelle?"

She wheeled around in surprise, cross with herself for having any feelings one way or the other about Lucca's personal life. "Yes?"

"When you're ready, I'd like you to come out and meet Stefana. She's the wife of my pilot friend Leo who was killed."

Annabelle's eyes closed tightly. "I—I'll be right there," she stammered as she tried to gather her wits.

*How awful for the other woman.* It hadn't occurred to her that this Stefana was here for any other reason than the seemingly obvious one. Annabelle had jumped to the wrong conclusion. Probably because she'd listened to the film crew make the odd remark here and there about Guilio's son being somewhat of a Casanova.

She imagined most attractive bachelors carried that same label. It went with the territory. But after their conversation last night, she had the feeling that if Lucca were ever to marry, he wouldn't be one of those rootless men who was easily distracted. Or was she only trying to convince herself.

Once she'd freshened up, she walked the rest of the way to the living room, which was decorated in authentic country Italian, if there was such a thing. Annabelle had only peeked in before now.

Lucca sat on a chair opposite Stefana, who was perched on a rose settee. He'd prepared them an elaborate lunch. It appeared they'd been together for quite a while. The moment he saw Annabelle standing in the doorway, he got to his feet.

"Come in, *Signorina* Marsh. I want you to meet Stefana Beraldi. I told her you're employed by my father."

When the other woman stood up, Annabelle could see she was pregnant. Probably six months. Her heart lurched because the baby would grow up without its father.

"How do you do, *signorina*," Stefana said in English with a heavy Italian accent.

"It's nice to meet you, *Signora* Beraldi. I'm so sorry

to hear about your husband. There really aren't any words, are there."

"No." Her brown eyes filled with liquid. "It's still hard to believe he's gone. I came to see Lucca. We've had a long talk. I asked him if he would be godfather when our little girl is born."

Being a godfather signified a great responsibility. Lucca's eyes traveled from her to Annabelle. "I told Stefana I'd be honored. She made this special trip from Naples to ask me in person."

She sniffed. "My husband and I talked about it the last time he was on leave. He loved Lucca."

"I understand Lucca loved your husband, too." Annabelle would never forget his sobs as he relived the horrific moment in the sky when Stefana's husband was shot down. She would be lucky to have Lucca for a lifetime friend.

The other woman smiled at him through the tears. "Don't forget. I'm planning on you coming for dinner after you're settled."

"I'll look forward to it."

"Good. Now I have to go."

"Let me see you out to your car."

Annabelle put her hand on the woman's arm, squeezing gently. "I'm glad you don't have too far to drive in your condition. Take care of yourself and your baby."

She nodded. "I will. She's all I have left of him." With tears streaming down her cheeks, she hurried off with Lucca. Annabelle watched from the kitchen doorway.

For a long time she'd wished she had Ryan's baby, even if their marriage hadn't worked out. But now she wasn't so sure. Stefana would have to raise her daughter on her own. How hard that would be.

It wasn't just the physical side of earning the living and seeing to the baby's every need. There was the financial and emotional drain of not having the father an intimate part of everything. Stefana would have to go through labor alone, shoulder the heavy responsibility alone. Unless she married again. But that could be a long way off.

Deep in thought, she watched the two of them converse a little longer before Stefana drove away. By the time Lucca came back in the house, lines had marred his face. The loss of Leo had taken its own toll.

"How long were you friends with him?"

"For the last five years."

"You two really had to be close for her to want you for the godfather of their child."

She saw the sadness in his eyes. "Being pilots together causes you to build a special bond. We were like brothers and talked about going into business together when we retired from the air force. But destiny had a different idea," he whispered.

Annabelle put a hand on his arm, desolate for him because the loss was a blow to his vision for the future. "Does his wife have family to help her?"

He nodded. "Lots of relatives. She phoned me yesterday and left a message. When I called her back and told her I was home from the Middle East, she begged to come over and see me."

"She's lovely. I have no doubts you'll make a wonderful godfather."

His eyes probed Annabelle's. "What would make you say that?"

"Do you really need me to tell you? How could you be anything else when you were her husband's best friend? I heard the love for him in your voice during your flashback. I'm sure he's up in heaven thrilled you're going to do the honors."

When she didn't think it was possible, a glimmer of light ignited those somber depths. "You're just what the doctor ordered today. How come you're home this early?"

"Our film crew worked fast this morning. Everyone wanted to get away to enjoy a long weekend." The word everyone included Annabelle, who couldn't wait to return to the farmhouse.

"Since my father flew to Milan this morning, does it mean you have no more calls on your time?"

"He did?" She wheeled around. "How do you know that?" she cried.

"I called him last night and told him everything."

She let out a happy gasp and wanted to throw her arms around him, but of course she couldn't. "Everything? Literally?"

"*Sì.*"

Her eyes misted over. "Thank heaven." The news that Lucca was home meant the timing for Guilio's surprise would have to be moved up. No wonder he'd gone to Milan today. He had to make new arrangements. His staff would have to work miracles.

"That sounded so heartfelt, I realize you really have been carrying a heavy burden. I admire your loyalty to my father. Very much in fact."

"He's a terrific man to work for."

Lucca's chuckle told her he had his own opinion on the subject. "We had quite a conversation about the beautiful *Signorina* Marsh. I told him I liked your company and want you to stay on."

She wanted that more than anything. It was a thrill to wake up in the morning and know Lucca was in the house, that they'd talk and fix food and just be together.

"Take your time to decide while you're enjoying your day off. What were you planning to do?"

A certain inflection in his voice convinced her he had to be at a loose end. "I thought I'd take a long drive and do exactly what I want to do."

She thought her response might have deflated him a little. Now that *Signora* Beraldi had gone, maybe Annabelle's company was better than none. Ironic that he'd craved his solitude, yet this week of being cooped up by himself was probably making him claustrophobic.

"Want to do it with me? You're welcome to come."

"I'm afraid I can't go swimming yet."

Even so, it sounded as if he would like to take her up on her offer.

"That's not on my agenda."

"I'm surprised." He gave her a speculative glance. "Most foreigners can't wait to ruin their complexions by tanning themselves on every beach they come to."

"Well, I'm not your typical tourist. Today I'd rather give my eyes a workout. Giovanni, the photographer, warned me not to get a sunburn or anything close to it." She flashed him a smile. "If you're interested, get what you need and meet me at the car."

When she went outside a few minutes later, she discovered him in the front passenger seat. With everything out in the open, she felt like she was walking on air.

Until now her dilemma had tortured her. Whose secret could be revealed first that would cause the least amount of damage? She knew enough of both men's past history to realize they were equally vulnerable. But now she didn't have to worry about it. Guilio's plan to surprise his son was still safe. The relief was exquisite.

Lucca turned to her, but she couldn't see his eyes for his sunglasses. "What's the verdict? Is my nurse going to leave me high and dry, or can I count on you to be around when I need to talk? Normally night is the time when I get my restless attacks. To know you're just down the hall gives me more comfort than you can imagine."

She sucked in her breath. "I'm still deciding." That was because the alarm bells inside her head were going off, warning her to proceed at her own risk. This was a man who already meant too much to her. Any more time spent with him, and he would become her whole world. But if he didn't reciprocate her feelings, then she was in for a letdown she might never get over.

He slanted her a glance. "I'm assuming there are times when you've had ragged moments since your divorce and need to unload on someone you can trust. I can be a pretty good listener if you'll let me."

There'd been times when she would have loved a confidant besides her parents. Lucca sensed it because he was a very intuitive man. It was also true that he'd needed help and their unplanned housing arrangement made it easy for her to provide it.

Annabelle didn't know when it had happened, but she did feel secure around him. For so long she hadn't believed she could depend on a man again, let alone want to. She'd thought Ryan's betrayal had caused a part of her soul to die, but Lucca's effect on her made her realize it had only gone into hibernation. Otherwise she wouldn't be taking this drive with him.

"You're like your father, hard to turn down."

"I like being compared to him, but it makes for fireworks when he and I are on opposite sides of an issue."

With a laugh she started the car and they were off. Lucca made a fabulous navigator and told her which roads to take for the most superb views. She chauffeured them through mountaintops and rows of grapevines blanketing the hillsides.

Hours later when darkness had fallen, they stopped for seafood at a charming fishing village outside Solerno, with its beach of black sand. The restaurant looked out over the water. People were dancing. Everything was perfect. Too perfect?

Afraid she was getting ahead of herself where Lucca was concerned, she didn't want to make a mistake that could be fatal in the end. Already she sensed he meant far too much to her.

"Isn't the fish to your liking?" He'd long since removed his sunglasses. His eyes traveled over her, taking their time.

"You know it is."

"Then why do you look…anxious? Surely you've been out to dinner with other men since your divorce."

"Only on business."

"Is that the reason you can't commit to staying on with me? Why do I get the feeling you're concerned my father's opinion of you will be altered in some way if you do?"

Annabelle stared at him over the flickering candle. Taking her courage in her hands she said, "Not just your father's. Yours, too. You see, I've come to revere both of you."

*Revere* was an interesting word, throwing Lucca for a loop. It went deeper than *like* or *admire*. Love didn't come into it.

Her eyes had flecks of violet among the blue. Right now they stood out. Lucca had noticed they did that when she was in a highly emotional state.

He was damned if he could figure her out. While they were eating, he'd been tempted to dance with her, but the doctor had told him not to do that kind of activity yet. To his consternation, the face and body that had lain next to his for that short time the other night had taken hold of his mind and wouldn't let go. After the time he'd been spending with her, he needed to feel her soft curves in his arms.

She smelled as good as the flowers surrounding the house. Better even, because she was a woman with her own feminine scent.

That time in the backseat of the car with her, the evening they did dishes together, the night when she'd arranged the pillows for his leg, he'd breathed in her essence. It filled him with longings more profound than those he'd felt with other women. He had the disturbing impression that one night's possession of her body wouldn't be enough for him.

The fact that he could admit it made him realize he was swimming in deep water himself. Never in his life had he been jealous of another man, but he suspected her ex-husband still had hold of some part of her heart. Otherwise she'd probably be married again by now or at least in a serious relationship.

She had that vulnerability about her that had brought

out his father's and Mel Jardine's protective instincts. She brought out more emotions in Lucca than he'd felt in the whole of his life where another woman was concerned. Before she bewitched him completely, he pushed himself away from the table and got to his feet.

His gesture startled her. She jumped up, too. "Are you in pain?" she whispered softly.

Yes. But not the kind she was referring to. He put some bills on the table. "A little. It seems I was so eager to spend the day with you, I left the house without bringing my pills with me."

A rose tint sprang to her cheeks. "Then we'll hurry back."

She turned and walked through the restaurant ahead of him, drawing the eye of every male in the place. Besides her long legs and other stunning attributes, her hair gleamed silvery-gold in the candle light, as if each strand gave off inner properties like the elements themselves.

When they reached the car, she opened the front door for him. The nurse in her proved to be ever attentive. Once he'd eased his sore leg in, she went around and started the motor. Was that all he represented to her? A patient?

The drive home didn't take long. Neither of them spoke. He waited until they were back in the house and he'd taken another pill. She was on her way to the bedroom by the time he called to her from the hallway. She turned around, eyeing him with what he thought was mild trepidation.

"I enjoyed today, Annabelle."

"So did I."

"Knowing how you feel about my father, you need

to hear that he ordered me to treat you like the princess you are. In other words, he gave his blessing because he has the highest regard for you and wants to trust me. With my reputation, which has had its moments of truth, I'm afraid I'm the one who has yet to prove myself worthy."

That brought a smile. "So far I can vouch for you."

His jaw hardened. "Don't count on that lasting too long. Would it shock you if I told you I'm a little frightened by the way you make me feel? *Buona notte.*"

Annabelle braced herself against the closed door, burying her face in her hands. *Lucca, Lucca.* Today he'd set her on fire with one look. Tonight at the restaurant when he'd helped her to the table, his touch had electrified her.

Given enough time she'd probably make an utter fool of herself with him. Intuition told her that once involved, she'd never want to get uninvolved. But she had to admit it was hard to walk away from him knowing he was still fragile.

Tomorrow morning she would move her stuff to the hotel before she left for the photo shoot. The pills always knocked him out. When he woke up, he'd see it was for the best.

Annabelle slept poorly for the rest of the night. Around seven she awoke after hearing a noise. She sat up in bed and listened for it again. Maybe Lucca hadn't been able to sleep and had gotten up to fix himself some lemon tea he favored.

There it went again, that mournful sound. An animal outside maybe? She threw on her robe. The minute she opened the door, she realized it was coming from Lucca's room. After listening again she realized he was in the middle of another nightmare. It didn't surprise her. Stefana's visit would have triggered memories from his subconscious. Unfortunately they'd found expression once he'd fallen asleep.

She tiptoed into his room. His covers were strewn on the floor. He lay on his stomach wearing nothing but the bottom of his sweats. Her heart ached to watch gut-wrenching sobs shake his body while his face was buried in the pillow. His hard-muscled physique was as stiff as an iron poker.

Without conscious thought she sat down on the mattress and curved one of her hands around his shoulder. The other went to his hip. "Lucca," she called softly to him. "Wake up. You're dreaming. Come on." Using a gentle rolling motion, she managed to get him on his back. More unintelligible words flew out of his mouth.

His tear-washed face was her undoing. She bent over him and started kissing his eyelids and cheeks. "Lucca?" she whispered. "You're no longer in the air force. You're home and safe." She ran her lips over every rugged line and angle of the face haunting *her* dreams. Her hands massaged his shoulders, willing him to relax and let go of the powerful flashback.

"Hush now," she murmured against his lips, both of theirs salty from his tears. "You're not alone. I'm here."

Just when she thought she wasn't getting through to him he muttered, "Annabelle?"

"Yes," she cried, so relieved he'd come back to reality, she didn't care what he thought of her unorthodox methods. Her sorrow for what he'd suffered went too deep for tears. He'd been injured and had lost his best friend. She rocked him in her arms. With a swift strength she could scarcely credit, he pulled her body all the way on to the bed.

"Your leg—"

"I'm being careful," he assured her. "Take off that nurse's hat and give me the kiss of life again so I know I'm not dreaming." In the next second his mouth covered hers and she found herself opening up to him. She couldn't hold back, not when she wanted him with such a hunger she was shocked by it.

Lucca had come awake, drawing long, deeply passionate kisses from her mouth until she couldn't breathe. They moved as one flesh, giving and taking their pleasure. She'd entered a realm of rapture she'd never known before and time ceased to exist.

Under his spell she was so far gone, she didn't hear the knocking on the kitchen door until Lucca relinquished her mouth with a groan and sat up to listen. He was more beautiful to her than any Roman god.

The knocking persisted even louder than before. "Someone wants to see you."

"Maybe its Basilio from work with a message from your father. It must be important, but I don't know why he didn't phone me. He has my cell number."

Embarrassed to be caught like this, Annabelle scrambled out of Lucca's warm arms and got off the bed, totally disoriented and disheveled. She could tell his morning whiskers had given her a slight rash.

"You stay here, Lucca. I'll see who it is."

His eyes were still slumberous from their passion. "Hurry back."

The huskiness of his tone set her body trembling. She shut the door to the bedroom and raced through the house to the kitchen, cinching the belt to her robe tighter around the waist.

"Who is it?" she called from behind the door.

"*Signorina* Marsh? It's Fortunato Colombari!"

Guilio's grandson. She'd never met him, but she'd heard about him. Taking a second breath she opened the door. A dark blond Italian teen, maybe sixteen or seventeen, stood there rocking back on his heels with a surprised look of undeniable male interest in his brown eyes. He stared at her for what seemed a full minute. Had he noticed her swollen lips, which Lucca had nearly devoured because they couldn't seem to get enough of each other?

"My *mama* sent me down to see if you require anything," he explained in very good English. "Guilio, my grandfather, is in Milan, so she agreed to watch out for you."

"How nice of her. It's a pleasure to meet you, Fortunato."

"Same here. *Mama* sent you some fresh melons. I will put them on the counter for you." Without waiting for permission, he walked inside carrying a basket of them. When she shut the door and turned around, her eyes saw what he could see.

Lucca must have been so tired last night, he'd pulled off his clothes and had thrown them over one of the kitchen chairs. His socks and shoes lay on the floor, one shoe on its side. Though he'd brought the dishes in from the living room, he hadn't cleaned up the kitchen after the big lunch he'd made for him and Stefana yesterday.

After almost staggering out of Lucca's bed and room, Annabelle had been so enthralled with him, she hadn't noticed anything else. But there was no doubt Fortunato was looking at everything and coming to the conclusion that she wasn't living here alone. And she was a messy guest, too.

"That was so kind of you to bring me fruit, Fortunato. Please thank your mother for me."

His eyes slid to the white cargo pants and blue sport shirt. He gave her a devilish grin. "I will tell her you are enjoying Italy very much."

She felt heat swarm to her face. *Guilty as charged.*

On his way out the door, he paused. "I will also tell her you are more *squisita* than Grandfather Guilio says you are. When the women in our family meet you, they will all be jealous and the men will wish they had met you first." He blew her a kiss. "*Ciao, signorina.*"

"*Ciao.*" She watched him drive away in a fabulous champagne-colored Amalfi four-door voyager.

"Sounds like you made a conquest of Ruggero's son." Lucca had come up behind her. His warmth enveloped her as his hands slid around her waist from behind. She felt his lips kiss the nape of her neck. It sent rivulets of desire through her body, causing her to gasp softly. But much as she wanted to go back to the bedroom with him and pick up where they'd left off, she couldn't.

"Lucca, he knows—"

"He knows a man is in the house," he said against the side of her neck and kissed her skin again. The mere contact made her feel light-headed. "He just doesn't know who. Once he tells his *mama* about the *squisita signorina* staying in my house, she'll be down to investigate.

"Does it matter? *Papa* knows I'm home." Lucca spun her around, wrapping his arms around her neck. "Now

I have to have this." He planted a hot kiss to her mouth, melting her bones in the process.

Annabelle could have stayed crushed against him indefinitely, but not wanting to get caught by Fortunato's mother, she tore her lips from Lucca's so she could ease away.

He studied her upturned features for a moment. "Don't be concerned. Fortunato is harmless."

"But he'll tell everyone what he saw and it will get out that *Signorina* Marsh has a lover."

"That frightens you, doesn't it?"

"Yes."

His black brows knit together. He grasped her upper arms. "Something tells me this has a lot to do with your ex-husband."

*"What?"*

A tiny nerve throbbed at the corner of his compelling mouth. "Some women feel guilty about enjoying another man even after they've been divorced. It usually means she still imagines herself in love with her ex-spouse and is waiting for him to come back to her."

"You may have known a woman like that, but that's an absolutely crazy theory and doesn't apply to me!" she cried.

"Doesn't it?" Lucca wouldn't let this go until he got the answer he wanted. "Ryan won't last long with the woman he's married to, even if they have a baby. You can count on it."

"Well you can count on this—examine my heart and you'll discover no trace of him there because he became extinct the day I learned he betrayed me."

He gave her a speculative stare until she wanted to

scream. In this mood, the passion they'd shared earlier might never have happened.

"Do you honestly think I would have switched hospitals, let alone have gone to work for Mel, if I'd still had the slightest hope Ryan would regret what he'd done and ask for a second chance? He destroyed every particle of affection I ever had for him."

Lucca gave an elegant shrug. "You've convinced me. I won't bring him up to you again."

"Thank you." Her voice shook.

"So what else is going on with you?" One brow had dipped dangerously.

"I don't know what you mean." Except she did because he always seemed to know when she was keeping something from him.

"I gave Papa my word where you're concerned. It seems to me you're more worried about your image with him."

She lowered her head.

Lucca heaved a frustrated sigh. "Let me tell you something about my father, Annabelle. If you were that kind of woman, he'd have seen right through you and he would never have asked you to model for him. You're someone very important to him. You must know that."

"I do. I just want those warm feelings to continue."

Everything Lucca said and did was making chaos of her emotions, but no one was as important to Guilio as his own son. One day soon he'd see what his father had done in his honor.

He brushed his lips against hers. "Let's get dressed and go down to the beach. I'll find one of my mother's sun hats for you to wear. We'll rent a cruiser and spend the day on the water."

She averted her eyes. "That sounds wonderful." Away from the farmhouse she wouldn't feel like they were sitting ducks.

The whole time she rushed to get ready, she feared there'd be another knock on the door. But when she walked through to the kitchen minutes later, he was there alone waiting for her with a covered basket.

Their gazes fused. "I made us a picnic."

"You're amazing. Have you got your pills?"

"Yes, nurse."

She ignored him and hurried out to the car to pop the trunk. He trailed her and put their things inside. When they were settled in the car, he smiled at her before putting on his sunglasses. "There's nothing like having my own driver and medic in one. I could grow to like this arrangement."

"Until the doctor tells a certain fighter pilot he has recovered enough to get behind the wheel of a car again."

When he laughed, Annabelle gave him a covert glance. "With rest and good food, you're walking so well, you're hardly recognizable from that first night." She drove out to join the road leading down to the major highway.

"You sound happy."

"I am." *I am.*

"Even though you had to supply comfort to a vet this morning?"

"Let's not pretend I didn't enjoy it after you woke up." *Enjoy* didn't cover it. "You proved to me there's life after death."

"That's nice to hear."

"Mel has been worried for me, but if he'd seen us together, those fears would have dissolved. That's your contribution, Lucca. Would you hate me if I told you I'm grateful to you for making me feel like a woman again?"

"I only kissed you a few times."

"It was enough for this relic to feel the heat."

She heard a harsh sound come out of him. He jerked his head toward her. "Is that how you really feel about yourself? How old are you? Twenty-five?"

"Almost twenty-seven."

"Don't you know what a beautiful girl you are?"

*Oh, Lucca.*

"I'm no girl." Yet his father had called her the Amalfi Girl.

"You're the stuff men's dreams are made of. Don't let what your ex did distort the truth. This morning I found out what a loving, giving woman you are. Don't tell me I don't know what I'm talking about because I was there with you."

She smiled. "I know. That means there's hope for you, too. For two survivors, we're not doing so badly after all. We've got a bit of a drive ahead of us to reach the marina. Tell me about your stepbrothers. What are their names again?"

"Ruggero and Tomaso."

"Do you like them?"

"Not in the beginning. We all had to live together in a villa farther up the mountain."

After losing his mother, Annabelle couldn't imagine how hard that would have been. "I didn't realize they had children as old as Fortunato."

"They were a couple of years older. I'm surprised my father hasn't told you all this."

She put on her sunglasses. "I think you're under the

impression I've spent loads of time with him, Lucca. But you'd be wrong. Guilio was only in Los Angeles two days. During that time we were in meetings with Mel. When I flew to Rome last week, he met my plane and it's been work ever since."

He rested his head against the window. "Have you met Maria?"

"Not yet."

"Aren't you going to ask me if I like my stepmother?"

"No."

"Why not?"

"Because I know how much you loved your mother."

"I adored her, but I've come to care a great deal for Maria."

"I'm glad." Wanting to know anything and everything about him she asked, "What's Fortunato's mother like?"

"Besides other girls, I dated Cellina before I joined the air force."

Out of the frying pan, Annabelle.

She swallowed hard. "Is she another reason you didn't want anyone to know you were home yet?"

"No." was his blunt answer. "You know my reasons. I didn't want my father to hear I was home before I could tell him myself. But to satisfy your feminine curiosity, if I'd been in love with her, I wouldn't have left Ravello."

Her fascination with him was so great, she couldn't stop asking questions. "Has it made things difficult for you and Ruggero?"

"Not anymore. But in the beginning I think my step-brother was glad I had a career that kept me away for long periods of time."

"I thought it strange she sent those melons."

"It's not strange at all." She felt his eyes impale her. "The whole family has to be intrigued by my father's sudden affection for the American woman he met in California."

The chemistry between them was palpable. "How about a little music?" She turned on the radio and grazed the channels until she found some soft Italian rock. After their conversation just now, she needed anything to help contain the feelings he'd aroused in her.

When she saw the sign for the marina, her heart leaped because they would be spending the afternoon alone on a boat. She pulled around past a string of launches and stopped near the office.

"I'll be right back." Before she knew what was happening, he cupped the back of her head and kissed her hard on the mouth. Annabelle was moaning by the time he finally relinquished her lips and got out of the car.

# CHAPTER SIX

On Monday morning, Lucca heard his father's car in the drive and walked out of the house to greet him. They hugged.

"You're really home for good. I can't believe it." They hugged again.

When Lucca had arrived at two in the morning last week, he'd been in such a terrible place emotionally, he couldn't have imagined feeling this good today.

"Come in the house, *Papa*. I've made *Mama*'s lemon tea for you."

"I haven't tasted that in years."

No. Lucca didn't imagine he had. "Everything's waiting for us out on the terrace." He'd prepared their favorite eggs, fruit, yogurt and pastry.

His father followed him. "You have a slight limp, nothing more. I thank God for that."

"I do, too. Once all the pain is gone, you won't even notice that. Come and sit."

Guilio looked around. Lucca watched his eyes glaze over. "Daisies on the table, just like your mother used to do. As if there aren't enough daisies surrounding the place."

Lucca fought his own tears. "How is your work going lately?"

His father rubbed his eyes before digging into his breakfast. "Your uncles and I can't complain. The good news is, we have a much larger market than we used to and need more help, but I know the family business has never been your interest."

"I'm glad it's growing, *Papa*."

His father chuckled. "You sounded like my little boy just then. I am, too. So…you're really decided on this farming business."

"Yes. That's why I want those two properties. Along with this one I plan to make a good profit. I intend for Cavezzali to sell the premier *frutta deliziosa* in all Ravello."

"This is your grandfather's doing."

"Only indirectly. I was born with some of *Mama*'s genes. She helped with the farming as a girl. I took to it pure and simply. But I also inherited some of your genes. You loved car design. I loved jet planes. It's all mixed around inside me."

His father eyed him for a long time, but for once Lucca couldn't discern what was on his mind. "You hated me for marrying Maria so soon after your mother died," he began without preamble. "I don't blame you. If I'd been in your shoes, I would have felt the same way."

Lucca was stunned by his father's unexpected re-marks. "We went over all this years ago. There's no need to talk about it ever again."

"Perhaps not for you as much as for me. As you know, Donata and I were childhood sweethearts. I loved your mother so much that when she passed away, I couldn't bear it for myself or you. Not many people loved the way we did. We had an idyllic marriage. When you came along after many tries, your mother looked at me and said, 'Our cup has run over, Guilio'."

"I didn't know she suffered a miscarriage."

"Four of them."

*Four?*

"We wanted a big family. I have to tell you she was the sweetest mother." *She was.* "You were our one and only. She doted on you. I think I was a little jealous." He wiped his eyes.

The revelations coming out of his father knocked Lucca back on his heels.

"I'd grown up knowing Maria at school and liked her. Her husband's sudden death from a heart attack was a shock to her, too. We saw each other at church. In our grief, we gravitated to each other for comfort to stave off the pain. We were two brokenhearted people with three brokenhearted sons and realized that if we got married, we could provide something solid for our children."

Lucca's eyes closed tightly.

"In the beginning our union truly was for the children." Lucca believed him. "We had friendship and respect going for us. Over time I grew to love her in a different way that I loved your mother. She's a good woman who has supported me in the business and has been a fine companion."

"Don't you think I know that? I care for her very much."

"But not at first. When you left for Bari, I got so angry because I didn't want to lose you, too. Your mother's death almost killed me. I wanted to keep you close to me, but the harder I tried, the more you pulled away." He got up from the table and walked over to him. "Can you forgive me, Lucca?"

Too choked up from emotion to talk, Lucca hugged his father. "If anything, I'm the one begging for it."

Guilio hugged him harder. "Maria and I have been planning a get-together on Saturday. Besides family, there'll be some friends and business people. Now that you're back, we'd like to turn it into a real 'welcome home party' for you. How does that sound?"

"I'm already looking forward to it, *Papa*."

His father wept. Lucca hadn't seen that happen since the doctor had summoned them into the hospital room where his mother was taking her last breath. But this time they were happy tears.

"Come on," his father finally said, wiping his eyes again. "Let's go take a drive and look at those properties. I'm glad you're going to do something about them and want to hear all your ideas. They're already an eyesore. That's why I wanted to sell them. Thank goodness you stopped me in time."

Thank goodness.


"The light is perfect. Annabelle? You will sit in the passenger seat with one foot on the ground as if you've fallen in love with this field of sunflowers and are ready to get out and run through it. Can you give me the look I'm after this early in the morning?"

That part was easy. The memory of Saturday on the water with Lucca was a day out of time with a real man who was starting to share his feelings. While they'd boated in and out of sandy coves and enjoyed their picnic, he'd given her a history of the area.

Against a backdrop of medieval towers and terraced orchards, he'd talked about his plans to become a farmer. With his love of the land, it really didn't surprise her. Slowly the conversation drifted to her. He got her talking about her own future. She knew that one day she'd go back to nursing. His words touched her deeply when he told her she ought to specialize in helping veterans because she had the two necessary gifts of empathy and compassion.

After he took his medicine, he eventually grew sleepy. She suggested they go back to the farmhouse so he could get to bed. After a day like they'd enjoyed, he'd seemed so peaceful, she had a feeling he wouldn't be tortured by nightmares.

Sunday had been a repeat of Saturday. Lucca was unwinding even more now. They ate a leisurely breakfast, then took another boat out in a different direction so she could see more sights and islands. Lucca lay on the padded seats, comfortable enough to enjoy being gone all day. They snoozed, ate, read and took in the scenery. She thought of them as healing days. For a little while they had no cares.

"Annabelle needs more apricot in her cheeks. I want her hair cascading over her left shoulder," Giovanni ordered, firing directions to the staff until he was pleased with the results. "See how the sun brings out the metallic gleam of those strands, Basilio?" The other man nodded. "With the bay of Naples sparkling in the background, that's the shot I want! Don't move!"

Annabelle marveled at the color coordination. A bright yellow Amalfi sports car convertible with creamy leather seats formed the centerpiece. Marcella had dressed her in a three-piece, short-sleeved crisp white suit and creased slacks. The jacket had four pockets trimmed with yellow braid.

The same trim ran up the openings and around the lapels. An enamel sunflower in each earlobe brought the color to her face. White sandals with elaborate criss-crossing straps completed the look.

"*Perfetto! Perfetto!*" Giovanni cried. "Now I want you to get out and lean against the car with the door still open, your left foot just so. You're holding this basket of sunflowers while lifting one to admire it. This time your smile holds a secret."

His directions unknowingly caused her body to break out in goose flesh. Earlier this morning Lucca was supposed to have made breakfast for his father. Right now she was holding her breath, dying to know how it had gone for both men. That was the problem with being a bystander. She was caught up in the lives of another family, yet could do nothing but hope it was a joyous one.

"That's not the smile I want, *signorina*. Where did the other one go?"

She fixed it for Giovanni. "I was thinking how hard it's going to be to leave Italy."

"Then don't! I'm sure Basilio will put in a good word for you with *Signore* Cavezzali if you want to stay. Now give me what I want!"

Annabelle tried her best. When he declared they were through shooting for the day, she was glad to get back to the van to change out of her clothes and remove her makeup. Once she was dressed in a blouse and skirt, she said goodbye to everyone.

Basilio reminded her they were doing the shoot in Ravello tomorrow. Relieved she wouldn't have to face another long drive in the morning, she got in the car. Before she drove away, she checked to see if there were any messages. Her body quickened when she saw that Lucca had called. She clicked on.

*"Papa and I have spent the day together and are out looking at the properties I was telling you about. I'm not sure how soon I'll be home.* Ciao, bellissima."

It sounded so much better than she'd hoped for.

She started up the engine and pulled out to the main road. Sorrento was sprawled across limestone cliffs where the houses looked like colorful children's blocks stacked on top of each other. Everything was beautiful along the Sorrentine Peninsula, but the drive was hot, even with the air conditioning on, and seemed to take forever.

As soon as she reached the farmhouse, she dove into work for something to take her mind off of Lucca and put in a wash. No sooner had she done that than she heard a knock on the kitchen door. Maybe it was Fortunato again. She hurried to open it.

*"Buon giorno, signorina.* I am Cellina Colombari. You met my son the other day."

Annabelle couldn't believe the timing. If she'd arrived a half hour later, she could have avoided this meeting. "Yes, of course." She smiled. "I ate one of the melons he brought. It was delicious and very kind of you."

Lucca's former girlfriend was probably in her mid-thirties. A real Italian beauty with dark blond hair and dark eyes. She must have gotten pregnant with Fortunato at nineteen or twenty.

"Can you stay and visit?"

"If it is all right."

"I'm through working for the day. Please. Come in."
She went into the living room and Cellina followed.
"Won't you be seated?"

"Thank you." She chose the rose settee. "When
Guilio said you were staying here by yourself, I thought
it might get a little lonely. I know I would be if I were
living by myself."

"Since my divorce, I'm used to living alone."

"That must be very hard for you. It's so sad. Basilio
lost his wife last year," Cellina informed her.

"So I understand."

"Do you find him good-looking?"

Annabelle knew where this was leading. Fortunato
hadn't wasted any time. "I think every male in Italy is
too attractive for his own good. Don't you?" She winked
at her.

The other woman looked surprised before she un-
bent and gave a soft laugh. "Yes."

Cellina might be too curious for her own good, but
she didn't take herself too seriously. Lucca would have
liked that about her.

"So tell me about you and your family. I'd like to
know a few things about you before I meet everyone at
the party Guilio has planned for Saturday."

They chatted for another twenty minutes, then
Cellina said she had to go and start dinner for her family. Annabelle liked her. She was glad the other woman
wouldn't be a stranger to her at the family party.

Lucca still hadn't called or returned. Unable to stand
her own company any longer, she left the house and
went for a walk. She almost forgot the floppy hat she
wore to keep the sun off her face and had to go back
for it.

When evening rolled around, she bought herself a cola, then geared up for the steep climb back to Lucca's house. On the way, her cell phone rang. It was Guilio calling!

She moved to the side of the road and braced herself against a palm tree, not knowing what to expect when she clicked on. "Hello?"

"Annabelle? You're a dark horse but I forgive you with all my heart for helping my son make the transition back to civilian life."

Her throat swelled. "You should have seen us the night he fell in the hallway."

"He told me about that."

"You must be so thrilled to have him back for good." Annabelle was overjoyed, not bothering to tamp down her excitement.

"You'll never know."

"Where is he now? Where are you?"

"One question at a time." He chuckled. "I dropped him off at the farmhouse. Now I'm home at the villa."

She gripped the phone tighter. "Is everything all right?"

"It couldn't be better."

"That's music to my ears."

"A lot of the reason for that has to do with you. Thank you for keeping my secret."

"I about died when he appeared out of the blue. I was so afraid he'd find out."

"Thanks to you, he didn't!"

"So what are you going to do?"

"I've got everything under control for the big surprise. I can't change the date of the grand opening in August. However, we can honor him at the party. When

I was in Milan, I moved up the date to Wednesday night and have informed Mel to change his flight arrangements. Your photo shoots will be over by then. We'll have a mini grand opening where my son will meet the Amalfi Girl in person when he's honored."

Only two days away... Though she'd been in Italy just a short while, she felt like she'd lived here much longer. The images filling her mind were suffocating her. His farmhouse felt like home. She and Lucca had lived in every part of it. Each room—the hallway...the terrace...the kitchen—had their own memories.

"I'll keep in touch with you about the details, but before we hang up, I just want to say thank you."

"For what?"

"Lucca's told me how you've nursed him. There's no one tougher than my son, but after what he's been through, he's more grateful than you know for what you've done. I have it on good authority he'd like to keep you until you leave. He says you're better than any nurse who has taken care of him since he was shot down."

Annabelle groaned inwardly. She'd hoped Lucca wouldn't want her to leave at all, but if he only thought of her as a nurse, and didn't care for her for her real self, she couldn't bear it. "I'm very flattered," she said in a wooden voice.

"He tells me that after you go home, you're thinking of taking up your nursing career at some point to work with war veterans like himself. My son has great admiration for you. Is that true?"

She stared blindly into space. "Yes, but I haven't said anything to Mel yet. That's something we'll have to discuss after I get back."

"Mel's not going to like it, but be assured my lips are sealed. I'll be checking in with you over the next few days. *Ciao,* Annabelle."

"*Ciao.*"

Feeling the happiness drained out of her, she clicked off, hugging the phone to her chest.

It was déjà vu when Lucca heard a firm knock on the kitchen door. If it were Annabelle, she had a key and could let herself in. She'd left her car in the drive and had obviously gone somewhere. A walk maybe?

She was constantly on his mind. Disappointed that she wasn't back yet, he walked through the house to the kitchen. The knocking persisted. "*Signorina* Marsh?" a familiar voice called out.

Fortunato again. He was a good kid. A little mischievous, but fun. So he'd come to see Annabelle again. The boy had good taste and eyes to see.

Out of his five nieces and nephews, Lucca had to admit he enjoyed him the most. Fortunato had this idea he would go into the military, too. None of the family was happy about it, and Lucca had never encouraged it. But at seventeen, a boy had his dreams. No one understood that better than Lucca.

He unlocked the door, surprising the life out of Fortunato. "Hey—when did you come home?" If Lucca didn't miss his guess, the teen sounded a trifle disappointed.

"I got in the other night."

"You did?"

"*Sì.*" He smiled. "Want to come in?"

"Yeah." After the door closed they high-fived each other.

"How's life treating you?" Lucca tossed him a plum from the fridge and took one for himself.

"It's okay." He squinted up at Lucca. "How long are you home for this time?"

"For good."

In a matter of seconds he'd surprised his nephew again. Fortunato looked perplexed. "I thought you were going to stay in the military until you retired."

"So did I, but my plans changed."

"How come?"

He gave his nephew the same answer he'd given his father. "Because I got injured and my priorities changed. I decided I wanted to do something different with the rest of my life."

"Yeah? Like what?"

"I'm going to be a farmer."

"You're kidding! You? A fighter pilot?"

"That's right. I've spent enough time in the air. Now I want to stay on the ground and get my hands dirty."

Laughter burst out of his nephew. "That's cool." Lucca finished off his plum while Fortunato looked around. "I saw *Signorina* Marsh's car in the drive. Is she here?"

"You mean the American who's working for your grandfather. She's probably still out with some of her coworkers."

"Oh." His face fell. "I met her the other day."

"Papa told me he'd hired her to do modeling for some of his ads."

"That's what I heard, too. She's one babe."

"But a little old for you, right?"

A ruddy color stained Fortunato's cheeks. "I bet she's no more than twenty-five. There's no harm looking."

"No. There's no harm in that." Lucca had done it himself, but not nearly long enough. In fact he planned to tell Annabelle what his nephew had said. She needed to realize she wasn't all washed up after what her ex had done to her.

Fortunato's blond brows lifted. When they did that, he reminded Lucca of Ruggero. "She's already got some guy hanging around."

"How do you know that?"

"I saw his clothes in here. You know…like they'd been partying and got carried away. She's only been in Italy a little while. He's one lucky stud. If I were just a little older…"

"But you're not." He reached out and tousled his hair.

"*Mama* thinks maybe it was Basilio."

"Basilio is a little too old for her, don't you think?"

"Not if she's after his money."

"I guess anything's possible."

"*Papa* says Basilio is gaga over her. It's all the talk at work."

"What's all the talk?"

"How gorgeous she is. You ought to see her, Uncle Lucca. Even you would have a coronary."

Lucca had already come close to having a heart attack and quite a few other things as well at the sight of the silvery-gold tigress ready to attack him with the cane that first night. He grinned at his nephew. "Even me, huh?"

"Yeah, well, *Mama* says you can get any woman you want."

Lucca hoped so, because he wanted Annabelle. "Aren't you working in the shop this summer?"

"Yeah. I have to be there at noon every day. Guess I better get going. Mama will have dinner ready."

"Do you want another plum on your way out?"

"Sure. Thanks."

"You're welcome." Fortunato was growing up in more ways than one. Little did Annabelle know she was his nephew's new fantasy, not to mention Lucca's. He watched the boy walk out to his car. "By the way..." he called to him.

Fortunato turned to him. "Yeah?"

Before shutting the door he said, "I'm the lucky stud whose clothes you saw lying around."

Annabelle let herself in the house and was clasped in a strong pair of arms. "At last," Lucca whispered, burying his face in her hair. "I've been watching for you. Where have you been?"

"Walking."

"I thought so." He pressed kisses all the way to her mouth. She couldn't deny that his hunger was as great as her own. Since his arrival in Ravello, they'd been thrown into an intimate situation. Lucca had never married and wouldn't be a man if he didn't want to enjoy his nurse until she'd gone. Annabelle didn't blame him at all.

*Thank you, Guilio, for the heads-up.* After their conversation, she was afraid she was in a different place than Lucca emotionally. Guilio had indicated Lucca valued her medical assistance. If that was all, then the trick was to be her wisest self until the party was over and she went back to California.

She eased herself away enough to talk to him and

cupped his face. "I have to know. How did it go with your father? He loves you so much."

His gaze wandered over her features in the semi-darkness. "Can't I tell you later? To be honest, all I've been able to think about is getting you alone." He began kissing the daylights out of her. Annabelle had never felt this alive before. Being with Lucca was like being reborn.

He started to maneuver her into the other room, but the fear that she would go on reading too much into his lovemaking prevented her from indulging herself for long. If he wasn't starting to love her as intensely as she did him, then she was playing with fire. Slowly she eased out of his arms.

"Why are you pulling away from me?"

"I didn't eat much today. Do you think we could go to dinner first? Then you can tell me everything."

Lucca's gaze swept over her. "I should have realized, but when I saw you come in the door, I only had one desire. Is there anything you need to do before we leave?"

"I'll just freshen up. Be sure to bring your pills."

He nodded. "I'm looking forward to the day I don't need them anymore."

"I want that for you, too."

After he'd held her back for another kiss, she hurried through the house to change clothes and run a brush through her hair. She put on the same sleeveless orange shirtwaist she'd worn the other day. On a warm night like this, the linen breathed.

When next she saw Lucca, he'd just come out of his room, walking toward her with barely a sign of a limp. He wore a pair of beige trousers and a silky white sport shirt, where she glimpsed the dusting of hair on his chest at the opening.

His sudden white smile sent her heartbeat skyrocketing. He was so Italian and attractive, she had to look down for a minute to get a grip. They left the house together and went out to the car. In the next instant he'd climbed in the passenger seat next to her.

"Hi." He leaned over and kissed her neck. The contact of his mouth against her skin radiated through her in waves. "Remember me?" The exact words she'd said to him last week.

"Yes." Her voice sounded all breathy. That was the way he affected her. She thought he was going to kiss her again, but to her surprise he squeezed her hand instead. "I don't dare do what I want to you right now or we'll never leave the farm."

"Maybe you should get in the back," she teased.

He drew in a harsh breath. "I prefer to be right where I am, up close and personal." So did she. Annabelle wished she could be more like Lucca and go with her feelings without dissecting it and imagining it taking on major significance. "What kind of food are you in the mood for?"

"Anything you choose. Surprise me." She put the key in the ignition and started the car, afraid to look at him directly. If she did, she'd beg to stay here and crawl into his arms.

"You're in a different mood this evening."

His radar never failed. "I think I got a little too warm during my walk."

"Then we need to hydrate you. I know a place not far from here." He gave her directions. After that, the pregnant silence on the drive to the restaurant passed in a blur because she was too conscious of his nearness and her susceptibility to him.

Every eating establishment on the coast was a scene of enchantment facing the sea. Lucca led them to a divinely romantic spot overlooking the water. He plied her with juice from the bar. Afterward they were shown to an individual terrace with a table for two, separated from the others by flowering trees for the diners' privacy. The blossoms gave off their own perfume. In the background a live band was playing Italian love songs for those who wanted to dance or simply listen.

After they'd been eating mouthwatering hors d'oeuvres automatically brought to every table, she found herself gazing into those gray-green eyes staring back at her between black lashes as silky as his shirt.

"I know the reason why you went away and joined the air force, Lucca. But if I'd been born in this particular spot on earth, I don't think I could have left it."

He finished the last of the olives the waiter had told them were freshly harvested from a nearby grove. "You have places in Southern California that rival our coast."

She shook her head. "No. Like these hors d'oeuvres I've been enjoying, places like Laguna Beach and La Jolla are merely appetizers compared to Ravello."

His eyes smiled at her. "That's a fascinating analogy."

"But true," she insisted. "On my walk, I stopped by the Villa Rufolo today. The place is an arabesque fantasy within a fantasy. With those enchanting gardens, it's no wonder Wagner was inspired for his *Parsifal*." She sipped her coffee. "I understand the Wagner festival will be on next month. You lucky people who live here."

"I prefer listening to Wagner when the town isn't overrun with tourists."

"I hear you." She smiled. "Southern California is like a wall-to-wall carpet woven of tourists. That's why I've loved staying in your home so much."

"You prefer it over the large villas?"

"They're lovely, but too big. There's a cozy warm feeling to your little farmhouse. The fruit trees and flowers surrounding it are like tufts of clouds, hiding it away from everyone. I'm crazy about it. If I were an artist, I'd paint it at various hours of the day."

"You mean like Monet, who kept turning out his poplar trees?"

She winked at him. "Exactly like that."

The waiter arrived with their fish entrée.

"I believe you're an artist in your soul," Lucca observed after they were alone again.

"I'm afraid I fixate on a subject rather than create from it." She'd fixated on Lucca from those very first moments and there was no antidote except to remove herself. "How did your day go today? Honestly."

"Honestly, my father and I are at peace. He told me he's behind my farming idea a hundred percent. And it seems he's decided to turn his business party into a homecoming party for me. But it's going to be on Wednesday instead of Saturday. I'm very touched."

"He's incredibly proud of you." Annabelle didn't know how she was going to wait that long for the big night to unfold.

As she looked at him, a mysterious gleam entered his eyes. "After Papa dropped me off, I had a visitor who looked shocked when I answered my own door. Care to make a guess?"

"Fortunato?" She'd almost said Cellina, but caught herself in time. Naturally the whole Cavezzali family had to be curious why Guilio had let Annabelle stay in his son's house.

He nodded. "I hate to have to tell you this, but the latest gossip has put you and the widower Basilio as an item."

She burst into laughter. "If your nephew had looked closely, he could have seen that your shirt and cargo pants would hardly have fit Basilio."

"He was too focused on you to notice details like that. I'm afraid he's smitten. That's when I informed him *I* was the other man in the house the other night. I could care less what conclusions he's drawn. According to him you couldn't be more than twenty-five."

"I don't believe it." She laughed.

"That's nice when you do that. For your information he's wishing he could make the stretch that would put the two of you into the category that you might treat him as a romantic equal."

"I'm afraid we've all been there before."

He leaned forward. "Who was Ms. Marsh's fantasy?"

"My art teacher in high school. He was probably forty, but I thought that was the perfect age for a man. He was so mature and self-assured. He made all the boys look pathetic in comparison. I used to think up reasons to hang around his class after school."

"You mean he let you?"

"Yes. Now that I think about it, it was pretty naughty of him."

Lucca's shoulders shook with laughter.

"Now it's your turn."

# CHAPTER SEVEN

Lucca gave her an unconsciously seductive smile. "Which fantasy would you like to hear about first? One of my father's secretaries, or the mother of one of my high-school friends?"

"Oh, brother." Annabelle shook her head.

"No fantasy ever looked better than the one sitting across from me." There was a tone in Lucca's voice and a look in his eyes that raised her temperature.

She took another drink of her coffee. "After Fortunato left, what did you do?"

He sat back in the chair. "Looked at the list of notations I've made of all the things that need fixing around the house."

"That's good you're staying busy."

His jaw hardened slightly. "You mean so I won't brood?" He'd jumped on her remark so fast, her head spun.

"No, Lucca. No…" she placated softly. "I didn't say that. You know I only meant until your pain was a little better."

"But you were thinking it. With good reason I might add. There are a lot of things I'd like to tackle, but for my leg."

"It's getting better every day." She knew that after a certain amount of work he got tired. That's when it started to hurt and made him edgy. "I've a hunch patience was never thy name, but you'll make it through this."

"I'd ask you to dance, but that's *verboten* for a time. So is driving."

"Lucca…haven't you listened to anything I've said? It's early days yet." Annabelle put the empty coffee cup back in the saucer.

A faraway look entered Lucca's eyes. "I've been dreaming too much about my plans for the farm. I want it too much."

"That's your pain talking. Remember you have a plate in your leg. That's making all the difference in your recovery."

"Why?" he snapped at her. Finally he was listening.

"You live with a constant ache and are probably dealing with some arthritis. The plate the doctor put along the side of your thighbone is helping bear your weight and has made early movement possible. However, the plate is shielding your bone from stress, which is not necessarily a good thing."

He sat forward. "Are you saying the doctor didn't know what he was doing?"

"No, Lucca…" She shook her head. "After your crash, you needed the surgery immediately to safeguard against further nerve damage. But because some stress on the bone is necessary to strengthen it as it heals, this stress-shielding has had some consequences, like your pain, for example."

His features broke into a grimace. "The news gets better and better."

"Actually it does," she assured him. "Considering that you experience pain when you're fatigued, I'd advise you to consult an orthopedic surgeon here and see if you're a candidate to have the plate removed at some point down the road."

She saw his hands close into fists. "If I thought I could get that thing out of there..."

"I know it's possible, but I'm not a doctor. Only he can determine if it's a procedure for you and how soon it could be done. If so, you could probably do most everything you used to do and be free of pain. If nothing else, it will improve the quality of the life you're living now."

He stared at her through new eyes. "You've given me hope I thought was gone."

"Hope is everything, isn't it? But if the doctor advises against it in your particular case because it could leave your bone with a residual weakness, I know you'll handle it. You're not an ace pilot for nothing."

She didn't have to look at him to feel his energy. Something earthshaking was going on inside him. "Do you want dessert?"

"After that fabulous meal, I couldn't eat another thing."

"Then let's go home, unless you've decided you'd rather stay at the Casa Claudia."

She wouldn't desert Lucca now. The possibility that something could be done for his leg meant he would want to talk about it. Since she'd brought it up, she needed to see it through.

"No. Much as I think it would look better to those on the outside, I'm afraid I've fallen in love with your house." *With you.*

"Good, because I already canceled your reservation and paid your bill."

While Annabelle sat there astounded, he got to his feet. She followed suit. There was a new gleam in his eyes.

"Papa had something delivered to the farmhouse earlier today. I'd like you to help me christen it."

Her heart thumped. "Subtlety isn't your strong suit."

One side of his seductive mouth lifted. "It's not a mattress, although that item is going to be next on my shopping list." He left money for the bill and ushered her out of the restaurant.

She walked out to the car with him. "The word *christen* has a definite connotation. I'm intrigued."

He squeezed her around the hip. "It signals that something new has been launched."

Lucca's choice of words reminded her of Guilio's plans for his fabulous new sports car. But she could hardly concentrate because Lucca was touching her and now her legs felt like mush.

"Sort of like your new life when you thought the other one was over after you landed in that war zone?" It was a miracle she could start up the engine and pull out on to the main road without having an accident.

His arm rested across the back of both their seats, creating havoc with her body. She felt him finger the ends of her hair. Electric currents shot through her. "That, and other things," he murmured, sounding the slightest bit cryptic.

"Shall we drive to Solerno for some more *torta*?" She couldn't take much more of his attention. It was driving her mad with desire. They needed to stay busy.

He angled his striking face toward her. "Are you

afraid to go home with me? The nerve at the base of your throat started throbbing before we got up from the table."

His eagle eye didn't miss anything. *You idiot, Annabelle.* He had to have eagle eyes to be a pilot, so it shouldn't have surprised her. "Maybe. Having agreed to stay with you, this is all new to me."

"Your honesty is refreshing." He tugged on a strand. "I promise not to do anything you don't want me to do."

"*Signore* Cavezzali—" Her mouth had gone dry. "We can't sleep together."

She heard him suck in his breath. "If you're telling me you don't want me, you'd be lying."

"I want you very much," she confessed with total candor. "But I'm sure your doctor told you it's too soon after your surgery."

"If he did—" Lucca's words came out like a growl "—I was probably too drugged to hear him."

"Then all the more reason to consult a doctor here. If this plate can be removed, then you don't want to injure what has been repaired to this point. It's not worth the risk. We can thank Fortunato for showing up before any harm was done the other morning."

She pulled into the drive and shut off the motor. Before he touched her, she sprang from the front seat, eager to see what he wanted christened.

Lucca moved ahead of her and opened the French doors to the terrace. "It's out here."

She followed him and looked to the left. "A swing!" It was long and roomy, just his size, with padded arms and extra cushions. The floral pattern matched the colors of the farmhouse's exterior. "How perfect for you!"

"For *us*," he corrected. "If you'll sit at this end, I can put my head in your lap and stretch my legs."

He had her royally caught, but it was where she wanted to be. As soon as she'd seated herself, he sat next to her, then lay down, extending his hard-muscled length where he could prop his feet on the cushion.

Lucca caught her hands and kissed the palms. "Since this is our favorite place in the house, I decided I wanted us to be comfortable. Our family used to have another one, but it got old and died."

The reality of Lucca made this her favorite place on earth. She looked down into his eyes and got lost in them.

"Come closer, Annabelle."

She needed no urging, but the awkward position made it difficult. "I have a better idea," she whispered against his lips. "Sit up for a moment." When he did, she slid off the swing. "Lie down so I can kiss you the way I want." She would indulge herself for a little while longer without hurting his leg.

Annabelle got on her knees and wrapped her arms around his neck. Their mouths fused at the same moment in an erotic explosion of need. No experience in life could have prepared her for this kind of ardor. The giving and taking transported her. His exploration of her features and mouth sent her into another realm of pleasure too exquisite to describe. She gasped softly because her emotions were brimming over.

He plunged his hands in her hair. "I could eat you alive, Annabelle."

She buried her face in his neck. "I thought that was what I was doing to you. It's a good thing I'll be going back to California soon. Otherwise you won't be safe from me," she joked, but was hoping with all her heart he might tell her he wanted her to stay with him permanently.

Instead he said, "Back to *what*?" He sounded upset. His free hand still cupped the back of her head.

"My job with Mel, at least for the foreseeable future. I'll have to ease him into the idea that I'm returning to nursing."

Still no hint from Lucca that he wanted her to be in his future.

She pressed a tender kiss to his lips. "Lie there and relax. This swing is perfect for you to lounge on. While you do that, I need to get ready for bed."

He frowned. "It's not that late."

Lucca needed company. She needed more than that. "It is for me. Tomorrow I have to be in Capri early. On my return I'll pick up some groceries and fix us dinner. How does *that* sound?"

By the expression on his arresting face, he needed appeasing. "You'll cook me something American?"

She kissed his jaw. "The kind of food my family loves."

That seemed to cheer him up to an extent. "When do you think you'll be back?"

"I'm not sure. Capri is only twenty miles from here, but with the traffic, it could be several hours." She kissed his lips. "I promise to hurry."

"If I'm not here, just let yourself in with your key."

Naturally he had his own life to lead. Now that he didn't need to worry about being seen, he could call on his family to get him around, or take a taxi. "Do you need anything before I go to my room?"

"Only you." He gave her one last ravenous kiss until she could hardly breathe.

It would be so easy to forget everything and climb on that swing with him. But she resisted the impulse and eventually pulled away. When she stood up, she had to rub her knees after being in that position for so long.

"You look comfortable lying there. Stay put and enjoy the beautiful night." She turned to leave, but he caught her hand.

"Please don't touch me anymore tonight," she begged.

"Just one more kiss to help me get through it. I don't mind being alone through the nightmares if you're there to bring me awake."

"Oh, Lucca." She had no will when he told her things like that. She leaned down and clung to him while her heart steamed into his. He'd become her whole world.

When she finally stood up, her desire for him was so strong that if he'd called her back, she would have stayed in spite of all her good intentions. But he didn't say anything… Was it because he was being the Italian male who still reserved a part of independence for himself?

She gave the swing a little push to rock him. "Good night, Lucca," she whispered.

"Sleep well, *bellissima.*"

Capri metallic blue described the Amalfi sports car gleaming in the sun. The white sailboat on the water formed the perfect backdrop. Even Annabelle could see that and she was no photographer.

The car had been parked at the Marina Piccolo. Annabelle found the little harbor enchanting and she loved the outfit Marcella had chosen for her. It was a white silk cheongsam with an all-over medium-sized print of flowers in various shades of blue. Heavenly.

Her hair had been put up in a loose knot, caught with real blue flowers. On her feet she wore a pair of high-heeled sandals in metallic white. Her wrist was encircled with three rows of light blue sapphires. The same sapphires adorned her ears.

"*Mama mia*—" Giovanni exclaimed when she stepped out of the van ready for the shoot. "You have never looked this beautiful before. I wonder why."

Lucca had everything to do with it. Her heart was bouncing all over the place.

Basilio nodded with a wide smile. "*Bellissima, signorina*. Bravo, Marcella! The Chinese style is *bella bella*. Annabella? Today you will stand at the front of the car with one hand on the bonnet, the one with the jewels. Look out toward the boat. You are waiting for your lover."

Annabelle got into position. She would give anything if Lucca were at the helm of that boat. When this shoot was over, she would swim out to him and kiss them both into oblivion.

"That's the look!" Giovanni cried a minute later. "Don't move!"

This morning she was definitely a woman in love. If that was the look Giovanni wanted to capture, he shouldn't have any trouble no matter which angle he wanted to take.

"With these photographs, Guilio won't be able to keep his calendars in stock." He moved around her snapping one picture after another.

She smiled. "Are you trying to butter me up, Giovanni? If so, you're doing a good job."

"You are the easiest model I ever worked with and you're not even a model."

"Nope, and I don't want to be one. I'm only doing this for Guilio."

"When his son sees this picture, he will fall instantly in love."

*How about permanently?* The words hadn't passed Lucca's lips. They might never.

"Hey, Annabelle—where did the Amalfi Girl just go? I want a few more shots."

"I'm doing my best." For the rest of the shoot, she focused on the meal she planned to make for Lucca.

"All right. That's it. Tomorrow we meet in Vietri at nine before the shops open and we're overrun with tourists. It will be our last day of shooting."

Annabelle was of two minds. Part of her couldn't bear for it to be over because it meant she had to go home to Los Angeles and leave Lucca. The other part was glad that the modeling would be over. She wasn't meant for this business. But she'd worry about that later as she raced back to the van to change and remove her makeup. She couldn't wait to get to the grocery store and do her shopping. When she stepped outside again in jeans and a pink T-shirt, Giovanni made a face.

"A woman who looks like you shouldn't run around dressed like any tourist."

"But I *am* a tourist. In a few days I'll be back in California doing my old job."

"Do you know how many would-be models would sell their souls to do what you're doing here?"

"Yes. Though it has been a wonderful experience for me, they are welcome to it. By the way, do any of you know if there is a supermarket around here? There isn't one in Ravello."

"*Sì*," Basilio said. "On the Via Matermania." He gave her directions.

She pecked his cheek. "Marvelous! Thank you, Basilio. A *domani*, everyone!"

Lucca saw the caller ID and clicked on. "*Prego?*"

"This is Dr. Cozza's office calling. The doctor is on the line."

"*Grazie.*"

"*Signore* Cavezzali?"

"*Sì*. Your nurse said you would phone me back when you weren't busy. I appreciate it."

"Sorry it's so late in the day. She told me about your surgery and the pain you've been having. That could be the irritation of the tissue from the plate causing tendonitis for example. Then again it could be caused by something else. There's no way I can make a judgment until I've seen you and taken X-rays. I have an opening next Monday."

"That's fine." Another week. Lucca would have to live with it. "But it *is* possible to have it removed?"

"Yes. In patients who have pain that is clearly coming from irritation caused by the metal, the chance of pain reduction is much more likely. However, you must keep in mind that if the pain is more generalized, and not clearly an irritation, the chance of pain resolution with the metal removed is more difficult to predict."

"I understand." Lucca gripped the phone tighter. "What are the risks?

"Obviously there are potential complications with this type of surgery. The most common problem is that.

metal removal can lead to a weakening of the bone where the implant is removed. Sometimes fractures form through the holes where the screws were implanted. But that may not have happened in your case and a certain amount of normal stress is necessary to keep the bone strong."

Annabelle had said the same thing.

"The point is we want to cut down on your pain and hopefully alleviate it all together. I'll put my nurse back on to give you a time for your appointment and I'll see you then."

"Thank you, Doctor."

He hung up, excited to tell Annabelle the news. For most of the day he'd been making phone calls to various contractors for bids. The house had sat empty for fifteen years and called for a lot of repair work to be done. The bathroom needed a total remodel into a master bath. He made a list of items he wanted replaced or installed, like a dishwa—

The phone rang before he'd finished the thought. He grabbed for it. When he saw who it was, his pulse accelerated to a feverish pitch. He clicked on. "Annabelle?"

"Hi! How are you?"

"I'm waiting for you. That's how I am. When can I expect you?" He didn't want to hear that there was a problem and she wouldn't be able to make it.

"I've finished the shopping and am on my way home."

"How long do you think that will be?"

"About forty-five minutes?"

He would have to live with that. "Make it a half hour."

"Hmm. You really are feeling closed in. I'll hurry."

"Not too fast. I want you to arrive in one piece. You're an excellent driver, but you're in Italy now."

"I've driven the freeways of California all my life and so far have lived to tell about it," she informed him with a laugh.

"That's not funny."

"I'm sorry. See you soon."

He clicked off, but it couldn't be soon enough.

Thirty-five minutes later, Annabelle pulled into the drive. He got off the swing and hurried into the house. Once he'd opened the kitchen door, he helped Annabelle with the groceries she was carrying. "It's about time you got here."

He put the bags on the counter, then reached for her. He must have taken her by surprise because she let out a cry. Her gorgeous violet eyes searched his. "I know I'm a little late. What's gotten into you? That's quite a welcome after the way you greeted me the first night we met."

"Forget that man. He no longer exists." Needing her like he needed air to breathe, Lucca crushed her against him and started kissing her in earnest. They were both trembling when he lifted his head.

Lucca couldn't take his eyes off her. She was the most beautiful sight he'd ever beheld. "What took you so long?"

"It's because the only corn you sell here is for the pigs and you can't buy it in a grocery store. I had to stop at a farm along the way. The woman said it was for the animals, but I talked her into letting me buy half a dozen ears. I heard her mutter something about Americans that I'm positive wasn't flattering."

Lucca burst into laughter. "You're fixing me corn on the stick?"

She laughed out loud. "Not exactly. It's called corn on the cob. Have you ever eaten it?"

"No, but there were some Americans guys I flew with who dreamed about eating it."

"Then you're in for a special treat."

"How can I help?"

"I need a big pot. Fill it a third of the way with water. I also need a saucepan filled halfway with water. Then I need a frying pan and masher for potatoes. Could you put some flour in a bowl for me and hand me the olive oil, pepper and salt?"

Lucca couldn't remember the last time he'd had so much fun. Maybe never. He got busy helping her. Within minutes she'd started frying chicken and peeling potatoes. Once everything was cooking, she drew out the corn.

"I'll cook four of these because I can't stop with just one corn on the cob. I'll want at least two, maybe more. This is called shucking."

He watched in fascination as she denuded the corn and dropped it in the boiling water.

"I bought butter for everything and some cream to mix in with the potatoes. We'll be ready to eat in a minute, then I want to hear about your day."

Before long, they sat at the table on the terrace. She watched with avid interest as he took his first bite of chicken and mashed potatoes. "Now butter and salt your corn and just start munching away."

When he'd eaten half the cob she said, "You've now had your christening of American food Annabelle-style. What do you think?"

"I'd tell you it was delicious, even if I didn't think it. But the truth is, it's delicious. All of it. You're a terrific cook."

Her full smile lit up his universe. "Thank you. Coming from the famous Chef Cavezzalli himself, that's a real compliment." She looked at him over her second piece of corn. "Judging from your mood, I take it this was a productive day."

He nodded. "Very."

"That's wonderful."

"So is your food." Not able to get enough of her mashed potatoes and chicken, he reached for the last of everything, including a fourth piece of corn. "Before you drove in, I was on the phone with an orthopedic man from the hospital in Naples. He's going to fit me in on Monday."

She went still for a moment. "For him to accommodate you this fast is the best news I've heard to date."

"If he can operate, I want you stay on and be my nurse. I realize Mel Jardine wants you back, but I need you more and will pay you whatever you ask."

That was twice she'd heard that Lucca needed her for medical assistance. She was afraid that what she needed from him wasn't in her stars, but it was a little too soon to tell him yes or no. The doctor might decide not to operate. It was possible Lucca wouldn't make a good candidate for the removal of the plate.

"Why don't we talk about that after you've had your initial visit with the doctor? In the meantime I want you to lie down on the swing and rest your leg while I do the dishes."

"I'll help."

"No, no. Have you forgotten the rule? Whoever cooks in this house does the cleanup."

Annabelle could understand why Vietri was called the pearl of the Amalfi Coast. The seaside village was dominated by St. John's 17th Century church. On the top was an elegant dome in majolica that stood out and provided the background for the shooting.

The rich jewel colors on an opaque white base forming the dome were symbolic of the art form developed by the artisans of Vietri. Their ceramics were sought by collectors from all over the world.

Guilio was supervising this last shoot. She had to admit she coveted the huge vase he'd chosen from one of the studios to place in the passenger seat of the sports car. It was worth thousands of dollars, decorated in colors of greens, oranges and browns on white.

The rich lagoon-green of the vase matched the painted green exterior of the Amalfi convertible. This model had been upholstered in a light tan to pick up the other colors.

Annabelle wore a sleeveless Etruscan print dress. A cape, denoting royalty, was fastened at the back of the shoulders and fell to the hem of the pencil-slim skirt. The outfit had been coordinated to match the design on the vase. Her light brown high-heeled sandals had straps wrapped to the ankle.

The hairdresser had taken a long time to form Annabelle's hair into braids, like the Etruscan women wore. The braids were caught at the back of her neck with a gold clasp. It matched the bracelets on her arms. These pieces represented some of the most fabulous jewelry she'd ever seen.

Marcella explained they were reproductions of Etruscan jewelry. Gold had been soldered to wide metal bands in hundreds of little dots. They glittered like gold dust in the sun.

For this shoot, her makeup had been applied in more dramatic fashion. They'd given her elongated eyes in darker eyeliner and she wore a dark bronze lipstick. The whole crew let out a collective cry of astonishment when she emerged from the van ready to pose.

"My dear—" Guilio walked toward her "—your hair rivals the jewelry. I knew you were the one to help me launch my new car, but not even I guessed how far you would surpass what I had in mind when I approached you."

Annabelle couldn't swallow for the emotion. "Don't tell me that now or I'll smear my makeup."

She noticed he had to clear his throat. "Today you're here on a buying spree and have stopped to pick up this treasure."

"Please don't ask me to hold it. I'd die if anything happened to it."

He chuckled. "Nothing so potentially dangerous. Pretend you've just bought it and are putting it in the car."

"All right."

The shoot began. Giovanni tried it from several angles and kept snapping away. Marcella rearranged the cape several times for the best effect.

Tourists had gathered round at a distance. They always did, but even with the security Guilio provided, they came closer than usual. When Giovanni announced he'd gotten the pictures he needed, the crowd broke into spontaneous applause. A lot of them wanted an autograph, but Guilio, along with the security people, waved them off with a smile.

She hurried back inside the van and began removing clothes and jewelry. Once that was accomplished, she got rid of the makeup, then checked her cell phone. She'd been hoping Lucca might have called, but he was probably busy with workmen who were supposed to be coming to the house today.

Heartsick because her days with Lucca were numbered if she went home, she emerged from the van sober-faced. Guilio had been waiting for her and picked up on it.

"Come with me. We have much to discuss and we'll do it over a late lunch. The seafood here is excellent. See that little restaurant farther along the sea wall? We'll just walk over there."

They both said goodbye to the crew. Within a few minutes he'd ordered scampi for them with scallops for hors d'oeuvres. He eyed her with affection. "Did you hear that applause today, and at the hotel in Amalfi?" She nodded. "We're going to be taking orders for so many cars, we won't be able to keep up with the supply."

"I hope so."

"I know so." He poured them a little wine. "Now let's get down to business. Tomorrow Marcella will come to the villa with her team to get you ready. You'll be wearing the outfit you wore during the shoot in front of the jet. We're going to do two launches. The big one in August is going ahead as planned with the media people from the television studios.

"Tomorrow night before dinner will be a sneak preview in front of the dealers and the family. It will be for Lucca, of course. I'll give my speech to honor him. We'll do it in the screening room with a slide show of all your shoots including today's.

"Giovanni is going to have to do a rush on this last shoot so it will be included. I'll explain that these slides will represent the pictures in the calendar we'll be sending out in August.

"When it's over, I'll ask you to come into the room and introduce you as the Amalfi Girl who will help launch the full-scale blitz in August. Be prepared to be besieged. The picture of you in front of the jet has been made up into three-by-five posters for them to take back to their places of business and display as a teaser. I'm afraid you'll be signing a bundle of them as the Amalfi Girl. Will that be a problem?"

"Of course not." He'd thought of everything and sounded in complete control. But Annabelle was pretty sure she had a fever. After worrying for so long about both men's feelings, the day was almost here. She didn't want anything to go wrong now.

"Maria phoned me while you were getting changed. She told me Mel is already at the villa. I'm sure you two have a lot of catching up to do."

Mel was already here? That was good. She needed to stay occupied until tomorrow was over. Surely when Lucca found himself the center of attention and realized what Guilio had been planning all this time, there'd be nothing but an Amalfi sun shining on his horizon.

"Since you refuse to relocate here and work for me in my office, you'll probably want to fly back with him when he leaves. It's entirely up to you, my dear. If I had my way, you wouldn't go, but you're too much like Lucca. No matter how much I might want it, I can't talk either of you into anything you don't want to do. You're your own people and I have to respect that."

He gave the waiter his credit card. When the other man returned, Guilio said, "Shall we go? I have a dozen details to attend to."

Guilio was so excited. She was, too, but when it was over, joy would go out of her life.

By the time Lucca had got up on Wednesday morning, Annabelle had already left for his father's villa. Lucca knew the homecoming party was a mixture of business and pleasure. He supposed Guilio had involved her in some way, but he was disappointed she hadn't told him her plans for today. He'd wanted her to go shopping with him, but it was evident he wouldn't be seeing her until the party.

Over the last few days she'd been preoccupied, even elusive at times. Much as he appreciated what his father was planning for him, he would be glad when it was over. With her no longer doing photo shoots for his father's ad campaign, Lucca was excited to spend whole days with her. Among many things, he wanted her opinion of where would be the best place to add another room on to the house.

At noon Fortunato came by to pick him up so he could buy a new suit. Since his nephew had recently got his driver's license, he jumped at the chance. After lunch at a teenage hangout, they did some shopping.

Lucca hadn't had a new suit in ages. He didn't like to wear them unless he had to. Guilio despaired of his son's preference for casual clothes. Tonight Lucca decided to surprise him and show up wearing something his father would approve of. Annabelle had never seen him in a suit, either.

Fortunato told him to go the whole route—new shoes, tie, shirt. The works. By the time they got back to his house, Lucca was tired. He hid the pain from his nephew. But when Fortunato drove off with the assurance that he'd be back later to pick him up, Lucca took some painkillers to ensure he got through the evening without anyone suspecting something was wrong.

Annabelle would know, of course. She noticed everything. He'd missed her so much he was half out of his mind.

"Hey, you look all right," Lucca teased his nephew when he came by for him at six.

"Yeah? You look spiffy yourself."

"Thanks. Your parents don't mind my borrowing you once in a while?"

"Of course, not. I heard *Mama* tell *Papa* maybe I'd stay out of trouble now. When are you going to go looking for a car?"

"I don't know. I'm trying to figure out what kind I want."

"Can I go with you?"

"Sure."

Fortunato grinned. "I want a sports car some day and race it along the Corniche. I love driving."

"And girls."

"Yeah. That, too."

Lucca chuckled and pushed him gently on the shoulder. "You're all right, Fortunato."

"She's going to be there tonight. I can't wait."

Neither could Lucca.

When they reached the villa, it turned out Annabelle

was nowhere to be found. After a while her no-show made Lucca feel as if he'd been punched in the stomach.

The family welcomed him en masse, as did the staff from the plant his father had invited. He gave Maria an extralong hug. Guilio worked his way through the crowd and embraced him. His eyes reflected pure pleasure when he took in Lucca's new suit.

"Now that you're here, we can get started. We're going to begin in the screening room before we have dinner out in the garden."

Lucca sensed something big was about to happen. His father was actually acting nervous, which wasn't like him at all. He followed him through the villa to the room his father had added on many years ago. He needed his own place to work and view his designs on a theater screen. This evening the room was packed with at least sixty chairs. Enough to accommodate everyone.

"You sit here, Lucca." Front row center.

As the others filed in, Lucca felt the hairs lift on the back of his neck. What in the devil was going on?

His father stepped back. "Tonight is really a twofold celebration. It represents two dreams of mine that have come to pass. The first is that my son Lucca would survive the war and come home for good one day."

Hushed cries of surprise and happiness broke out from the family seated around Lucca.

"The second has to do with the first. You see, I thought he wouldn't be coming for a visit until August. But he surprised me, forcing me to move up my timetable two months for the surprise I've been planning in his honor for over a year."

*What?*

# CHAPTER EIGHT

"Years ago I saw the design for a sports car in my dreams. Amalfi has never made a sports car. Except for my wives, Donata and Maria, no one else knew about it. Once it was perfected, I shared it with the engineers and a prototype was made."

His father's eyes found Lucca's. "I've called it the Amalfi MB-Viper after the fighter jet Lucca has been flying in combat. I want my decorated son to know how deeply proud I am of him for serving his country so well and nobly. It is a great honor to be your father, Lucca. If your mother could be here tonight…"

The room broke into clapping. Everyone stood up and cheered. It went on and on. Lucca sat there in disbelief, absolutely stunned by his father's tribute.

"*Grazie, Papa.* I'm overwhelmed," he said in a husky voice.

"Welcome home, *figlio mio.*"

Lucca stood up and approached him. Deep inside of him he felt gratitude that he could walk up to him on both legs. After kissing his father on both cheeks, he put his arm around his shoulders and faced the audience. "Every son should have a father like Guilio Cavezzali."

"Hear, hear," everyone shouted.

"I wouldn't be surprised if *Mama* can see what you've achieved, *Papa*, but she couldn't be more proud of you than this son. I'm thankful you're my father, and I'm thrilled to be home with you and Maria." He gave his father's shoulders a squeeze before going back to his seat.

After a few minutes of thunderous clapping, the din finally subsided and people sat down. Guilio had to clear his throat several times.

"Tonight you're going to see the Viper's unveiling through a slide show. These photographs will go into calendars you will receive in August when the cars go out on the market. Every client who buys one will be given a calendar. Believe me, the calendar will do the word-of-mouth advertising for you.

"The launch will take place in Milan with total media coverage. Those of you dealers here tonight are getting a sneak preview. I'll send posters back with you. They're made up from the cover of the calendar. Basilio? If you will turn off the lights and start the show please."

Lucca had to blink back the moisture glazing his eyes several times while he tried to focus on the theater-sized screen. Suddenly there was a larger-than-life photograph in living color of a fabulous, gleaming white sports car convertible parked in front of an actual fighter jet. The lines were fantastic. His father had created a true masterpiece.

But dominating everything for Lucca was the jaw-droppingly gorgeous woman draped across the pearly-looking upholstery, twisting her delectable body just enough as if waiting for the pilot to come and join her.

*Annabelle!*

The blood pounded in his ears.

He could tell the picture had been taken at twilight at the air base outside Rome. His thoughts flew back to that first night in the hallway of the farmhouse when he'd vetted her rather cruelly and she'd said she'd just come from there.

Her skin gave off that magical glow. She was wearing a deep purple cocktail dress with spaghetti straps and a diamond necklace around her throat. A matching diamond bracelet was wrapped around her wrist. Her semicurly hair gleamed a silvery-gold over one shoulder. Her eyes shone pure violet.

She was so bewitching, he was dumbstruck. So was everyone else. A hush had fallen over the room. At first there was total quiet. After a moment he heard cries of "bravo" followed by heavy clapping and more cheers. Everyone got to their feet in tribute. They went crazy, as much for Annabelle as for the car.

In his gut he knew a poster of this photograph would be sold by the hundreds of thousands throughout the world. His father had known what he was doing. It filled Lucca with a deep sense of pride at Guilio's colossal achievement. The knowledge that he'd named the sports car to honor Lucca's choice of career was so humbling, he couldn't find the words.

Several of the dealers called out to Guilio in excitement. Soon the questions were flying at him. They wanted to know where he'd been hiding this breathtaking model. Who was she? Would she be visiting the different dealerships? Would she pose for pictures with them to put on their own websites?

The agreement was unanimous. Sales would skyrocket and they all wanted to meet the woman who'd made the launch of this magnificent car a transcendent moment. Guilio simply answered with a mysterious smile.

While Lucca was still trying to recover from the emotions bombarding him, another photo appeared on the screen. There she was, exactly like she'd been that first morning on the terrace, wearing that broad-rimmed hat and white eyelet sun top. The shot had been taken at Positano.

She sat in the black sports car with its black leather upholstery while she gauged the steepness of the terrain. Her appeal reached out to the audience like a living entity. A completely spontaneous, ear-splitting ovation broke from the crowd.

While Lucca was clapping with them, a third photo filled the screen. It showed her reaching for a cluster of grapes growing in a vineyard at the side of the road in Furore, Italy's own version of the hanging gardens of Babylon.

She was more luscious than the purple fruit that matched her eyes. She wore a cream-colored outfit and leaned against a light jade version of the sports car. Lucca sensed every male in the room wanted to catch hold of her jade scarf and pull her out of the screen into his lap.

He studied the photograph, marveling at the amalgamation of his father's creative engineering genius and nature's flawless design of womanhood in all her springtime glory. Everyone sat there mesmerized. A man could be forgiven for buying the car in order to own the photograph that came with it. Lucca could guarantee the calendar would become a collector's item.

As the next picture lit up the screen, all the oxygen seemed to be sucked out of his lungs. At the side of the gleaming yellow sports car, Annabelle held a basket of sunflowers picked from a whole field of them reflected behind her. They'd shot this in Sorrento. In the three-piece white suit with yellow trim, she looked good enough to eat.

It reminded him of the morning she'd picked the daisies pushing through the grillwork of the terrace. Like his mother, she responded to his world of growing things. He felt his whole body and soul respond to this woman who in a very short time had become a living part of him. The idea of not being able to wake up to her every morning for the rest of his life was unthinkable.

The photo taken in Vietri nailed him to his seat. She looked like some exotic Etruscan princess come to life who was so damn beautiful in those braids, he was hypnotized. You could believe the rich green sports car was her personal chariot. The sight brought another chorus of bravos from the crowd.

His father's exceptional vision had found Annabelle clear across the ocean.

*What exactly do you do for my father, Signorina Marsh?*

*I'm helping him with his ad campaign.*

Guilio had brought her to Italy and now his finished product had been translated into something wondrous to behold. Not until this evening did Lucca fully appreciate his father's expertise that would blow every other car off the road once it hit the market. With Annabelle's help, he would succeed in triple spades.

Still staggering from the impact of so much beauty, his eyes fastened on the shot of her dressed in a cheongsam, looking out over the waters of Capri from the side of the metallic-blue sports car. He'd been to China many times, but he'd never seen beauty like hers.

With each photograph, the energy in the room had become electric. The talk had grown louder as they reacted to what they were seeing.

"I saved December's photo for last," Guilio finally said.

Oohs and ahs came out unsolicited as every eye was riveted to the bride at the footsteps of the church in Amalfi with the flame-red sports car parked below her. The sudden explosion of excitement in the room went over the top. Everyone was on their feet shouting congratulations to Guilio.

But Lucca couldn't move from the chair. His lungs were frozen at the exquisite sight of Annabelle in that gown and mantilla. He couldn't make a sound. He'd had a complete physical before coming home from the hospital, but wondered if his heart could withstand this.

"Basilio?" his father called out. "If you'll turn on the lights, I'd now like to introduce you to the woman in the photos."

As the lights went on, Lucca turned in time to see her make her entrance from the back of the room. She was wearing the purple cocktail dress and diamonds. The whole room burst into stunning applause and stood to clap as she walked up to a smiling Guilio.

Lucca's gaze took in her tremulous eyes, then the other parts of her, bit by gorgeous bit, until it fell to those fabulous legs where the frothy purple fabric danced and teased him.

He watched his father put his arm around her shoulders. "Annabelle Marsh is from Los Angeles, California. She works for Mel Jardine, my best dealer in the States, who's here tonight. Annabelle is my not-so-secret weapon anymore." Everyone laughed. "She's going to put the Amalfi MB-Viper on the map. Ladies and gentlemen? May I present, the Amalfi Girl!"

When the applause finally died down, Guilio quickly led Annabelle out through a side door to escape the crowd. As soon as it closed, she gave him a hug. "I know this night meant everything in the world to him."

His eyes watered. "I know it did, too. For both of us. Thank you again for not giving my surprise away."

"As if I would have!"

He wiped his eyes. "It would have been understandable. My son had to have been dying of curiosity since he arrived at the farmhouse. It's just a miracle you could keep it from him."

"It was brilliant of you to move up the date of the party. He had to know something unusual was going on. As for your car, it's sensational, Guilio. I listened in the back during the slide show. Every dealer was bowled over with excitement to start selling them."

"Let's hope the sales reflect my belief that we have a winner here."

"You're too modest. You already know it is."

"And you're too kind." He walked her over to a table. "We've put you out here so you can sign the posters. People are coming through now. I'll be back in a little while."

Annabelle sat down, looking out on the garden. The lights had been turned on, transforming it into a fairyland. Guilio's new sports car sat on a raised platform. It was the one in flame-red. The dealers could examine it, climb in it, check out the engine and take home a brochure with all the specs printed.

While she was looking for Lucca, one of the dealers came up and asked for a signature of the Amalfi Girl. At that point a line started to form. For the next while she was besieged just as Guilio had predicted. While she answered dozens of questions, she wrote on each poster as fast as she could, losing track of time.

"Sign mine 'from Annabellissima,'" instructed a deep, beloved voice.

She threw her head back and discovered Lucca's grey-green eyes staring down at her, liquefying her bones with his intimate gaze. He'd dressed in a formal light grey suit and tie. She didn't know a man could be that handsome. His eyes swept over her in a restless motion, missing no curve or detail about her. Blood swarmed into her face, making her go hot.

"Lucca…" she whispered in an aching voice.

"I can't find words, either," came his husky admission.

She knew what he meant because the sight of him robbed her of breath. Her fingers curled around the marking pen. "Maybe now you won't be as upset with me."

He cocked his dark head, gazing at her through shuttered eyes. "Upset?"

"You know—for begging you to let your father know you'd come home early."

"With a divine surprise like this, how could I be?"

"I'm so glad this night finally came. He wanted everything to be perfect for you."

"It *was* perfect. *You* made it perfect. Now I want my own autograph from you."

The way he said it in that deep tone sent a thrill through her sensitized body. She unraveled one of the posters and signed it in the bottom right corner. When she'd finished, he rolled it up and tucked it beneath his arm. The look in his eyes set her trembling.

"You have no idea how hard it was not to tell you what your father was planning. Please don't take this wrong, but under the circumstances, it was a good thing you couldn't drive a car yet. Otherwise—"

"Otherwise I would have followed you because I couldn't have helped myself and curiosity would have killed the proverbial cat."

"Yes." She laughed softly.

"My father knew what he was doing when he stole you away from Mel. More than the fact that you're incredibly beautiful, you didn't let him down. After watching the slide show tonight, I'm convinced you could have a career as a top model."

"Those are heady words, *signore*, but for now I like being Mel Jardine's assistant at the showroom in L.A. when I'm not nursing." She'd leave Italy with a smile on her face if it killed her. Looking at the Italian soldier she loved to the depth of her soul, it already was killing her.

*"Signorina Marsh?"*

She jerked her around. Since Lucca had come to the table, she hadn't been aware of anyone else. "Hi, Fortunato!"

He broke into a broad smile. "Those pictures were fantastic. You look fantastic! Would you autograph the rest of these posters for me? I'm going to give them to my friends. They're going to eat their hearts out when they find out I know you."

Annabelle chuckled. "You know how to make an old lady feel good."

"Old lady—are you crazy?"

"Thanks, Fortunato. You've made my night. I'd be happy to sign these." She felt Lucca's hot gaze on her while she autographed the last six for his nephew.

"Thanks." He gathered them up and turned to Lucca. "Do you want me to drive you home now?"

She held her breath while she waited for Lucca's answer. "That's very nice of you to offer, but Annabelle's going to drive us back to the farmhouse. Here." He pulled some bills out of his pocket and put them in Fortunato's hand. "I owe you for today."

He stared at the money. "What's this for?"

"For chauffeuring your old uncle around town and showing me the hottest clothes to buy. See you later."

"*Ciao.*" Fortunato's eyes lingered on both of them before he disappeared.

"He's darling," she remarked.

"Ruggero says he's incorrigible, but I couldn't ask for a nicer nephew." He shifted his weight. It made her wonder if his leg had started to ache. "Do you have to stay around here much longer?"

"No. I'm through. Your father will be talking business half the night. I'll go inside the villa to change and meet you at the car in the courtyard. Give me ten minutes."

"Make it five."

"I don't think that's possible."

"Try." He sounded out of breath. "While you're gone,

I'll gather up some food for us from the party and we'll eat when we get back to the farmhouse."

His male virility was so potent, she'd forgotten all about food.

The blood surged through her veins as she left the table and rushed inside the villa. Marcella was there to relieve her of her clothes and jewels. She hugged Annabelle.

"Because of you, my shop in Rome will be besieged by women wanting to look just like you. Of course that's impossible, but it's the thought that counts."

Annabelle burst into laughter. "Thank you for everything you've done. I know Guilio is very grateful."

"You were a delight to work with."

"I'll never forget you, Marcella."

After she left, Annabelle removed her makeup and tied her hair in a ponytail. Once she'd slipped into pleated khaki pants and a light blue cotton knit top, she hurried back outside.

Lucca stood by the car, holding the door open for her. There weren't words to describe his looks adequately. She felt like a frump in comparison, but kept a smile pasted on.

"The Amalfi Girl is gone."

"No." His eyes traveled over her before coming back to her face. "The real Amalfi Girl is standing in front of me, the one my father saw when he went to California."

"Incredible, isn't it?" She got in the car and waited for him to go around and get in the other side. "He said he saw my bones and knew I was the one he wanted."

"My father has a visionary side to him. The other side is the persuasive businessman."

She started the motor and drove down the gravel drive to the road. "I found that out."

Lucca's hand slid to her thigh and gave it a gentle squeeze. "I'm not going to apologize for touching you like this. After the way I saw all the dealers devouring you with their eyes, I'm feeling possessive of you. Since I came home, we've lived in our own private world and I've grown to crave it."

What he'd just said had silenced her. In the palpable quiet that followed, his cell phone rang. Annabelle bet it was Guilio wanting to talk to his son. It was only ten o'clock, but she knew Lucca's leg was hurting. He'd been at the party long enough to start feeling uncomfortable.

He gave her leg another squeeze before removing his hand to answer it. She expected to hear him talk in affectionate tones to his father, but there was silence. She glanced sideways at Lucca and her spirits fell. There were long periods where he listened, then spoke in low tones. Annabelle couldn't make anything out except that his body had tensed and that wasn't a good sign.

After he hung up, her anxiety increased while she waited for him to tell her what was wrong. By now they'd reached the farmhouse.

"That was Stefana Beraldi's mother calling from the hospital in Naples."

Uh-oh.

"Stefana started bleeding earlier in the day. She was rushed to emergency hoping the baby could be saved, but it wasn't possible. It seems she's in the operating room right now having some kind of procedure done."

"A *D* and *C*," Annabelle said quietly.

"What is that?"

"An abbreviation for a dilation and curettage. Sometimes tissue remains in the uterus and it has to be removed."

Lucca grimaced. "Her mother said she'd be in the hospital for another twenty-four hours. I've got to go to her."

"I'll drive you now, but before we leave here, I'll run inside for your pills. Don't move. By morning you're going to be exhausted and will start hurting without them."

When she came back to the car a minute later with his pills and a couple of colas, Lucca had pulled some ham-and-cheese rolls from a sack. He handed her one with a napkin. "After the day you've been through, you need to eat first or you'll be too tired to drive."

She finished hers fast and drank half her cola before starting up the car once more. Lucca devoured five in a row and swallowed all his drink before settling back against the seat with a heavy sigh.

"Why did this have to happen to her?" The bleakness in his tone caused her to groan inwardly. To hear this awful news after the wonderfully unforgettable night...

Annabelle drew in a shaky breath. "One obstetrician I worked with told me a miscarriage can mean something was wrong with the baby and it wasn't meant to be, but I realize that won't be of any comfort to Stefana."

He turned toward her. "Do you know my mother had four miscarriages before I was born? I only found that out the other day."

"Your poor parents. How hard that had to have been on them, but especially your mother. With every conception, all the hopes and dreams start up. Thank heaven she was able to carry you to term."

A harsh sound escaped Lucca's throat. "Now Stefana's hopes are dashed."

"She'll mourn the loss for a long time because it has followed on the heels of losing Leo, but it won't last forever."

"I won't know what to say to her."

"There isn't anything to say. Platitudes don't help at a time like this. What she needs is for people to be there for her, Lucca. Seeing you, drawing from your strength—that will do her the most good. She'll probably want to talk about her husband because you were with him at the end. It'll do you good to mourn with her too. There's comfort in doing that together. One day she'll get better."

Lucca moved his arm to the back of the seat. She felt his fingers massage the nape of her neck. "Are *you* better, Annabelle?" he whispered. "Some people say divorce is worse than death for a spouse."

*Not since I came to Ravello.* Annabelle wanted to say those words aloud, but then Lucca could be in no doubt how she felt about him. Until he spoke the words she needed to hear, they'd remain unsaid.

"It's true my divorce left a void because my husband took up space. But I feel fine. Who would want a rootless man who isn't capable of love? You taught me that."

He reached for her hand and grasped it. "Did you want a baby from him so badly?" He was terrified for Stefana.

"I thought I did, but with hindsight I can see I wouldn't want to raise a child alone. In time Stefana will meet another man and have babies with him. Wait and see."

Annabelle didn't tell him that to a girl growing up,

the idea that one day she'd become a woman and carry the child of the man she loved was part of what a woman believed was her rite of passage. To see him in her child, to see his smile or his eyes, or the way he walks or laughs—that was a woman's dream.

To have Lucca's babies, to watch for his traits in them—for Annabelle *that* would be one of the ultimate joys of marriage to him. But she feared it wasn't going to happen.

It was seven in the morning when Annabelle pulled into the drive of the farmhouse. The visit with Stefana had drained Lucca. Upon leaving the hospital, he'd taken three pain pills because the pain was worse. Ten minutes ago he'd fallen asleep. She'd almost gone to sleep at the wheel herself.

Somehow she managed to wake him long enough to get him to his bedroom. She undressed him down to his suit trousers, then made him lie down so she could pull off his shoes and socks. After adjusting the pillows between his legs, she started to draw the lightweight cover over him and felt him tug on her arm.

"Don't go away," he begged, sounding drugged. "I need you next to me."

To appease him, and herself, she curled up next to him. His arm automatically went around her and pulled her closer, as if they'd been doing this for years. She was in love with this man, the heart-wrenching kind you never got over. To lie in his arms all night was her dream, but he was in a deep sleep and most likely wouldn't waken until afternoon.

When next she had cognizance of her surroundings, she heard her cell phone ringing. It came from her purse, which she'd put on the dresser when they'd come in. Carefully she slid off the bed and made a grab for it, afraid it would waken Lucca.

She hurried out in the hall to a kitchen filled with daylight. One glance at the caller ID showed it was her boss. She'd assumed it was her parents, whom she'd neglected for the last few days during the rush to get ready for the party.

"Mel?" Her mind was so blank, she had trouble gathering her wits. "Hi! How are you?"

"More to the point, how's the Amalfi Girl this afternoon?" She looked at her watch. It was one o'clock. She'd slept close to six hours. Lucca was still out for the count and probably wouldn't stir till later in the day.

"I'm back to being Ms. Marsh."

He laughed. "Lovely as she is, that's good to hear. I miss my assistant. Guilio and I had a long talk at breakfast with his staff. He said he was through with you until August. He said he felt guilty to have kept you away from me this long. But not too guilty obviously." Mel chuckled. "Since I'm flying out of Naples at five this evening, do you want to fly home with me?"

No. No. No. No.

"Annabelle? Are you still there?"

"Yes."

"For a minute it went so quiet, I thought our call had been dropped."

"I thought the same thing," she said.

"If you're going with me, it means we'll have to be at the airport by three at the latest. Because of traffic, Guilio said we'll need to get going within the hour. He's going to drive us to the airport. On the way he'll tell you all the wonderful things everyone said about you."

She'd just come from Naples. She'd spent all night with Lucca. How could she just leave?

*How can you* not, *Annabelle!*

Her work was done here a few days earlier than originally planned.

Lucca and his father had enjoyed the long-awaited reunion. They needed time to cement their new relationship. He was starting on his remodeling plans for the farmhouse. He had a doctor's appointment on Monday to see about his leg. The man had a new life to put together, plans to make.

Except for him to want her as his nurse, at no time had he talked to Annabelle about a future with her. If he'd ever told her he was in love... If he'd ever said he couldn't live without her... He'd had opportunity after opportunity. Though they'd discussed her future, he hadn't indicated he wanted to be a part of it, or her to be part of his.

She left a note on the terrace table for him.

Dearest Lucca. I've enjoyed this unexpected interlude with you more than you can possibly imagine, but interludes by their definition always come to an end. Ours is over, but I'll never forget. The Amalfi Girl is gone until August, when I'll be resurrected for the media blitz. I hope to see you then. Annabelle.

Steeling herself not to peek in on Lucca and kiss his mouth one more time, she stole out of the farmhouse with a heart heavier than the bags she'd packed. After closing the door behind her, she took off in the car with her purse. With a whole family ready to wait on him, Lucca would be perfectly taken care of.

Before she reached the villa, she phoned her parents, who were still up watching television before going to bed. They were overjoyed to hear she was coming home and told her they would pick her up at the airport. Her mom wanted her to stay with them for a few days, but Annabelle told her she had to get right back to work Monday morning.

She adored her family, but right now she was in too much pain to be leaving Lucca to think about anything else. Once she'd gotten off the phone, she had to pull over to the side of the road because she was sobbing so hard. Emotions she'd been holding back began to pour out of her. She didn't know if she could stop.

In truth she felt more married to Lucca than she'd ever felt with Ryan and they'd only been together a week. When the worst of her paroxysms had passed, she wiped the tears off her face and lifted her head.

She needed to get going, not daring to hold up the men. For the first time since she'd been in Italy, she wished her makeup woman were here to give her a fresh face, but all that was over and Annabelle would have to make the repairs herself from now on.

*Just like Stefana, you're going to have to find a way to go on, Annabelle.*

# CHAPTER NINE

DR. COZZA motioned Lucca over to the screen to see his X-rays. "I've been through your file. The doctor who operated on you did an excellent job. I see no fractures. It appears the pain you're having is local."

He turned off the light and looked at Lucca. "I can take your plate and screws out right away." The news elated him. "I believe it's the right decision to prevent deterioration and stop the stinging. Some people don't realize this procedure can be done and they wait years. Your doctor didn't tell you?"

"He probably did, but I wasn't listening at the time. Actually it was a friend of mine who's a trained nurse. She said it was possible."

"You're lucky she was so on the ball."

Dr. Cozza didn't know the half of it. "This isn't too soon?"

"No. You were operated on close to four months ago. You're good to go. Let me talk to my nurse." He stepped out of the examining room while Lucca paced the floor. Before long he came back. "I have an opening on Friday morning. You'll have to be here by five-thirty to get prepped."

"You can fit me in that fast?"

The doctor smiled. "I make room when my patient is a returning war vet hero."

"*Grazie*," Lucca murmured with heartfelt gratitude. That was only four days away. Lucca's mind reeled. "If all goes well, how soon can I get back to regular activity?"

"Two weeks on crutches, more to give the incision time to heal than anything else. You'll need someone to help you. Then you can throw the crutches away."

"Does that mean I'll be able to drive and swim?"

He nodded. "And have sexual intercourse. That's the greatest concern of all my patients with your kind of injury."

After they shook hands, Lucca left the hospital and climbed in the limo he'd hired. He instructed the chauffeur to drive him back to Ravello. He called ahead to the villa and was relieved when Maria told him his father was busy in his office off the screening room, working out the details of the media blitz he was planning. After telling her to expect him, Lucca stared at the view, not seeing it because Annabelle's image got in the way.

After waking up at four on Thursday afternoon and not finding her there, he'd called the villa, assuming she was having a conference with his father. When Maria told him she'd left for the airport with Mr. Jardine to fly home to Los Angeles, he almost did go into cardiac arrest. Then he saw her message on the patio table that left him shocked and then hurt to the quick.

At that point it had been too late to reach her by phone. She'd already boarded the plane. By the time he figured she'd touched down in California, he'd decided it was best to leave her alone until he'd been to the doctor. When he knew anything about his condition and prognosis, then he'd know what to say to her.

"Lucca, come on in," his father exclaimed when he saw him in the doorway. He got up to give him a hug and kiss him on both cheeks. "Do you have any idea how happy it makes me to know you're just down the hill and can drop in on your old dad when you feel like it? Sit down. Tell me what's on your mind."

He explained about the new surgery planned for Friday, delighting his father that this operation could take away his pain altogether.

"Do you want to recuperate at the villa, or would you like me to find someone to care for you? Whatever suits you best."

Lucca's heart thudded. "I want Annabelle back."

"*Grazie a Dio!*"

They stared at each other with a perfect understanding.

"Would you lean on Mel Jardine before I phone her?"

"You know I'd do anything for you."

"Right now?"

His father broke down in laughter. "I've been waiting for the day when my bachelor son finally went running the right way."

Annabelle waved to the salesman who'd been popping in and out the last few days to tell her they were glad to see her. But it was surreal to be back at the dealership. The receptionist out in front was doing her job. It was business as usual around the dealership.

"Line three for Colin.

"Line seven for Rick. Your party's been holding for five minutes."

"Line two for Annabellissima."

The receptionist pronounced Lucca's name for her like Annabellisthmus. She almost fell out of her chair from shock.

Trembling in every atom of her body, she picked up the phone. "H-hello, Lucca?" she stammered.

"I've needed to hear your voice. It's felt like months."

*Years.* She'd been praying for this. Her eyelids squeezed shut. "How are you?" She could hardly talk.

"Nervous."

Her hand tightened on the receiver. "Why?"

"I saw the doctor today. He's going to perform surgery on my leg Friday morning. He says I'm going to need help for two weeks. I don't want anyone else but you around because you're the only one who understands about all my problems. Do you think your boss would let you come for a medical emergency? I'll prepay your airline ticket."

Annabelle didn't have to think. After talking to her mom the last few days, she wondered if she hadn't made a mistake leaving Ravello so fast. What if Lucca had been waiting to have a serious talk with her? If so, Annabelle hadn't given him a chance.

"Hold the line for a minute and I'll ask him." She lay the receiver down and raced into the adjoining office. Mel was on the phone. He gestured her to come all the way in and sit down until he was through.

She was too emotional to sit. He finally hung up from his call. "What's going on? I've never seen you pace before."

"Mel? Lucca just phoned me. He's still on the line." In the next breath it all came out in a gush.

He smiled. "I can hardly deprive him of a good nurse

when I once had the best. Will you at least wait to fly back until Wednesday? I need your help with some matters backed up around here. You're the only one who can sort them out."

"Thank you!" She hugged him around the neck and hurried back to her office. "Lucca?"

"*Sì*? You sound out of breath."

"I had to run to his office." But that wasn't why she was close to hyperventilating. "He says I can come. I probably won't be there until Thursday. It all depends on my flight schedule."

"Let me know the time and I'll send a limo for you."

"Thank you." After a pause she continued, "Lucca…?"

"I can't wait to see you. All that's important now is that you're coming back to me. *Ciao*."

The doctor told Lucca the third day after surgery would be the worst. Maybe it was, but with Annabelle waiting on him, he didn't notice it as much. It certainly couldn't compare to the pain he'd suffered the night he'd come home and had fallen in the hallway.

"Uncle Lucca? Annabelle wants to know if you're hungry for dinner."

Fortunato had been a constant visitor in the evenings after he'd got off of work. He'd let him lean on him in and out of the shower. Lucca welcomed his nephew's help.

When the two-week recuperation period was over, Lucca would be helping Annabelle into the shower, only one of the many things he planned to do with her. Tonight he planned to open up to her, but he was nervous. That, more than anything, had put him off his food.

"Maybe some grapes and a roll."

"I'll tell Annabelle, then I've got to go. Carlo and I are going to a soccer match."

"That sounds fun."

"Not really. Our team's going to lose."

"Maybe you'll meet a cute girl there."

"You mean one who looks like Annabelle?"

Since there was no chance of that, Lucca didn't say anything

"Did I hear my name taken in vain?" She breezed into the bedroom carrying another vase of freshly picked daisies and put them on his dresser.

Fortunato grinned. He wasn't the only one who enjoyed looking at her dressed this evening in jeans and a jade-green blouse with cropped sleeves. Lucca could feast his eyes on her indefinitely.

"Uncle Lucca wants some grapes and a roll. Now I'd better leave or Carlo will have a fit. See you tomorrow. Thanks for dinner, Annabelle. You're not a bad cook."

"You mean for an American."

"I was just teasing. Those fajitas were awesome! You'll have to teach *Mama* how to make them."

"Fajitas?" Lucca questioned.

"Mexican food," she explained. "You take strips of steak, peppers and onions stir-fried in a special sauce. Then you roll it all up in a flour tortilla. I brought a couple of cans of them in my suitcase to fix a different kind of meal for you."

"Yeah, Uncle Lucca. Too bad you don't feel good enough to try one."

"Maybe tomorrow," Annabelle said. "For such a lovely compliment, you can come over anytime, Fortunato."

"Thanks for helping me," Lucca called after his nephew.

Soon they were alone. Annabelle's smile faded as she stared at him. "You're not hungry, are you."

"Not particularly. Why the concern?"

"Maybe it's the new painkiller you're on. I'll call the doctor in the morning and see if he'll prescribe your other one. You need to eat."

"It's not the medicine."

"So you admit there's something wrong."

He heard the alarm in her voice. "Yes. There's been something wrong for a long time, but I couldn't speak about it until now."

She stood by the bed looking nervous. "What is it?"

"I've never asked a woman to marry me before. If I can't have you, I plan to remain a bachelor for the rest of my life because you've spoiled me for anyone else. I'm not going to give you any time to think about your answer. Do you love me?"

A cry escaped her lips. "How can you even ask me that? I'm desperately in love with you. It's why I came back." The love-light in her eyes almost blinded him.

"Don't come any closer. My heart can't take it when I'm lying here incapacitated right now. I love you, Annabelle Marsh," he said, his voice throbbing. "I want to put my roots down with you so thick and deep, you'll know this is for real and forever."

She nodded.

"First we have to get married. Just as soon as the doctor gives me a clean bill of health. How about at the church we pass between my farmhouse and the villa?"

Her beautiful blond head nodded again. "Is that the one you went to with your parents?"

"Yes. I'll fly your parents and family over. You don't know how eager I am to the meet the people who raised such an angelic daughter."

She crept over to him and sat down, burying her face against his shoulder. "My parents will adore you. They won't believe the beauty of this place."

"Have you told them much about me?"

"I guess I'd better admit to the truth now, because you'll hear it from Mom when you meet her." She leaned over to kiss him.

After kissing her back he said, "What truth?"

"She's been worried about me for a long time. But after you and I clashed in your hallway, I phoned her and told her I'd met a man who'd already changed my life. And if I was lucky enough, maybe I would change his. I kind of told her you looked like a god with black hair and gray-green eyes. I also said Dad would be jealous because when my mom first met you, she would go weak in the knees and might faint, just like me."

Lucca laughed quietly before rewarding her with more kisses.

"You're my beloved, Lucca. I'm so madly in love with you, if I lost you now, I'd want to die!"

Lucca couldn't take it in. "You're my life, *adorata*. After your confession, I guess I can tell you mine. The night you came at me with the cane, I knew somewhere deep inside you were the woman I'd been waiting for all my life. But I was terrified because I wanted to be ready to give you all the things you deserve. I feared that after what you'd been through with your first husband, you wouldn't be able to trust me."

"Darling…" She traced his profile with her finger.

"You have a lot to learn about a woman in love the way I am with you."

"I'm finding that out," he said in husky voice. "Now I've got another question."

She read the anxiety in his eyes. "You mean about being a farmer's wife? I can't wait! Do you know something? I guessed that about you right from the beginning."

He looked surprised. "How?"

"I actually pictured it in my mind that first morning sitting on the terrace. You'd just crept back to this farmhouse in the dead of it because you're a home boy at heart. Your mother and her family had a love for the earth and all the beautiful things that grow here. Though you have a lot of Guilio in you, you're an extension of her and your grandfather."

She nestled closer. "When I got into bed that first night, before you fell in the hall, I felt that the family who'd once lived here had been supremely happy. Through all your pain and suffering, I saw how much peace the farm gave you. Your eyes would go soft when you looked around. The sight of the daisies I picked seemed to speak to you."

He nodded. "My mother used to pick them in the morning and bring them in house, just like you did."

"What a wonderful memory you have of her. When you made tea from the lemons growing outside, I learned something profound about you and could imagine you out pruning the trees. I could see myself watching you, coveting your body from a distance while I thought up ways to lure you back in the house."

"Annabelle," he whispered, his voice raw with

emotion. "Keep saying things like that and never let me go."

"As if I could," she cried, covering his mouth with her own.

"This is Canale Eight, with the six o'clock news, broadcasting live from Milan. Tonight ladies and gentlemen, we're at the Amalfi main showroom in Milan where Guilio Cavezzali, CEO of the one of the most prestigious lines of cars in Italy, is about to unveil their latest creation."

Annabelle sat in the driver's seat of the black-on-black sports car, knowing the television camera would be on her the second the curtain was drawn. All she had to do was drive the car into the center of the showroom and follow Guilio's lead.

Her hair had been swept to one side and cascaded over one shoulder to reveal diamond earrings and a diamond choker. Marcella had decked her out in a stunning flame-orange cocktail dress in a chiffonlike fabric. The straps went from the center of the bodice and fastened at the back of her neck. Her high-heeled sandals were covered in diamondlike brilliance.

Lucca was out on the floor with Maria and Basilio, watching Annabelle from a distance. He'd dressed in a silky black shirt and tan trousers. Her gorgeous husband ought to be the one in the spotlight. She happened to know the black model sports car with the million-dollar price tag was his favorite.

As soon as she got the cue from one of the guys, she started the car and drove to the spot where she'd practiced several times to get it right. Guilio stood front and center with a microphone.

"Here comes the Amalfi Girl now. You'll see her picture in all our showrooms around the world. Tonight we are happy to announce the launch of the first convertible sports car our company has ever designed. I've named it the Amalfi MB-Viper in honor of my son, who served our country flying one of the Viper fighter jets.

"She'll get out and open the hood so you can zoom in for a closer look."

Guilio gave a rundown of the impressive stats as Annabelle stepped from the car with as much as grace as she could and did the honors. So far so good as she moved from spot to spot, demonstrating the car's features.

Even from a distance she noticed Lucca's eyes smolder as he watched her walk around and open the passenger door to point out the luxurious upholstery and dashboard.

Finally her father-in-law smiled into the camera. "From zero to sixty miles per hour in three seconds. Take a drive in the MB-Viper and slide silently into the future."

With those words spoken as the new slogan, the filming came to an end. After a year or more of planning, the night Guilio had dreamed about was over. Much as Annabelle had been willing to do this favor for him, she was glad she wouldn't have to do it again. But thank heaven he'd approached her that day in California. Otherwise she would never have met the love of her life.

After the film crew cleared up their equipment and left, Lucca walked over and put his arm around her. "You were a vision up there," he whispered against the side of her neck.

"Thank you, darling."

"You were superb, Annabelle." Guilio had never looked happier. "To show my appreciation, I'm giving Lucca the car and you the diamonds for your wedding presents. Marcella wants you to keep the dress you're wearing as a memento of this night."

"I'll never be able to thank you enough for having faith in me. But most of all—" her voice caught "—I thank you for bringing your wonderful son into the world."

Lucca's eyes gleamed as she kissed his father and Maria on either cheek. Later she would thank the designer. "Basilio? No one could have been easier to work with. Thank you for your patience."

"It was a pleasure, my dear. The whole staff, Giovanni especially, sing your praises."

"Thank you."

Lucca was right behind her to embrace his father and stepmother. Then he stunned her when she heard him say, "Would you two mind making sure our bags go back on the plane with you? I've got plans for my bride and me."

Before she knew what was happening, he'd ushered her back to the car and helped her in the passenger side. "Enzo?" he called from behind the wheel to one of the staff. "Would you be good enough to open the bay door for us? I've a need to show off my unique driving skills to my gorgeous wife."

Everyone laughed before he backed them out of the showroom onto the outside lot. He shot Annabelle a mysterious smile before revving the smooth quiet engine. Suddenly they wound around to the main arterial and were whizzing through the streets of Milan.

Annabelle's heart steamed into her chest. Her gaze

fixed on Lucca, who drove with an expertise befitting a fighter pilot. "Where are we going?"

"Home."

"You mean all the way to Ravello? In this car?"

His smile melted her bones. "That's what it's for."

"I know, but we didn't bring anything with us. I'm still dressed like the Amalfi Girl!" Her silvery-gold hair radiated out in the warm August night air.

"Since she'll never be seen in public after tonight, I like the idea of driving around with every man's fantasy. Don't look now but you've already stopped traffic."

She blushed. "Lucca..."

"It's true. The guy in the other lane was staring at you so hard, he just rammed into the back of a truck."

"You made that up."

"If you don't believe me, turn around." His hand reached out and clasped her thigh. He liked to do that a lot. Every time he did it, the contact made her gasp in pleasure.

"I think you'd better keep both hands on the wheel, darling."

"Don't ruin things now and tell me you're going to be a backseat driver."

Her eyes filled as she looked at him. "I'm so happy, I'm in pain."

"So am I, but it's the best kind."

"*Lucca*—"

"There's a charming palazzo not far from the city. We'll stop there for the night where I plan to ravish you and hopefully get you pregnant."

Her heart thudded. "Promise?"

A half hour later they pulled into the grounds and

parked the car in a private garage that led to their own luxurious apartment. She hurried inside, sick with excitement. They'd been married several weeks, but every day with him was like the first day. Making love with him had become necessary to her existence.

After he closed the door, he pulled her back against him and slowly removed her earrings and choker, kissing every spot his lips could find. She moaned deliriously as he undid the back of her dress and turned in his arms, sensing his urgency. He crushed her against him until their bodies pulsated as one entity.

Annabelle didn't remember being carried to the bed. They no longer had to worry about his leg. This was her husband loving her with the kind of hunger she couldn't have imagined before meeting him.

"I love you," he cried. "I can't get enough of you, *bellissima*."

"Now you know how I feel." Her heart surged as their mouths and bodies began giving and taking, whipping up their passion until they spiraled out of control. He brought her joy beyond comprehension.

Later, when they were sated for the time being, Lucca reached for the remote and turned on the television. "The ten o'clock news will be on in five minutes. I want you to see what you look like from the audience's viewpoint."

She rested her head against his shoulder. "You'll have to translate most of what the TV announcer says." She'd been working on her Italian, but it was going to take a lot longer to master his beautiful language. When the film segment came on, Annabelle couldn't relate to the woman in the black sports car.

"It was terrifying to be live on camera. I was praying I wouldn't make a mistake, or fall on my face."

He pulled her closer. "You were sensational. My father looks good there, too."

"You both have intrinsic class. Not every man is so blessed. It's a quality you have to be born with. My mom remarked on it the day of the wedding." She hugged him tighter. "Didn't you love our wedding?"

"Yes," he whispered. "The only thing missing was my mother. She would have loved you."

Annabelle kissed the tears that moistened his eyelashes. "I'd like to think she was there to help your father give you away to me for safekeeping. I made vows then, and I'll say them again now. I, Annabelle Marsh Cavezzali, promise to take care of you and love you all of our life and beyond, my dearest, darling husband, Lucca Cavezzali."

\* \* \* \* \*

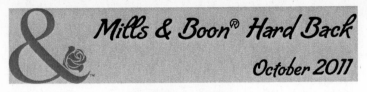

*Mills & Boon® Hard Back*

*October 2011*

# ROMANCE

| | |
|---|---|
| **The Most Coveted Prize** | Penny Jordan |
| **The Costarella Conquest** | Emma Darcy |
| **The Night that Changed Everything** | Anne McAllister |
| **Craving the Forbidden** | India Grey |
| **The Lost Wife** | Maggie Cox |
| **Heiress Behind the Headlines** | Caitlin Crews |
| **Weight of the Crown** | Christina Hollis |
| **Innocent in the Ivory Tower** | Lucy Ellis |
| **Flirting With Intent** | Kelly Hunter |
| **A Moment on the Lips** | Kate Hardy |
| **Her Italian Soldier** | Rebecca Winters |
| **The Lonesome Rancher** | Patricia Thayer |
| **Nikki and the Lone Wolf** | Marion Lennox |
| **Mardie and the City Surgeon** | Marion Lennox |
| **Bridesmaid Says, 'I Do!'** | Barbara Hannay |
| **The Princess Test** | Shirley Jump |
| **Breaking Her No-Dates Rule** | Emily Forbes |
| **Waking Up With Dr Off-Limits** | Amy Andrews |

# HISTORICAL

| | |
|---|---|
| **The Lady Forfeits** | Carole Mortimer |
| **Valiant Soldier, Beautiful Enemy** | Diane Gaston |
| **Winning the War Hero's Heart** | Mary Nichols |
| **Hostage Bride** | Anne Herries |

# MEDICAL ROMANCE™

| | |
|---|---|
| **Tempted by Dr Daisy** | Caroline Anderson |
| **The Fiancée He Can't Forget** | Caroline Anderson |
| **A Cotswold Christmas Bride** | Joanna Neil |
| **All She Wants For Christmas** | Annie Claydon |

*Mills & Boon® Large Print*

*October 2011*

# ROMANCE

| | |
|---|---|
| **Passion and the Prince** | Penny Jordan |
| **For Duty's Sake** | Lucy Monroe |
| **Alessandro's Prize** | Helen Bianchin |
| **Mr and Mischief** | Kate Hewitt |
| **Her Desert Prince** | Rebecca Winters |
| **The Boss's Surprise Son** | Teresa Carpenter |
| **Ordinary Girl in a Tiara** | Jessica Hart |
| **Tempted by Trouble** | Liz Fielding |

# HISTORICAL

| | |
|---|---|
| **Secret Life of a Scandalous Debutante** | Bronwyn Scott |
| **One Illicit Night** | Sophia James |
| **The Governess and the Sheikh** | Marguerite Kaye |
| **Pirate's Daughter, Rebel Wife** | June Francis |

# MEDICAL ROMANCE™

| | |
|---|---|
| **Taming Dr Tempest** | Meredith Webber |
| **The Doctor and the Debutante** | Anne Fraser |
| **The Honourable Maverick** | Alison Roberts |
| **The Unsung Hero** | Alison Roberts |
| **St Piran's: The Fireman and Nurse Loveday** | Kate Hardy |
| **From Brooding Boss to Adoring Dad** | Dianne Drake |

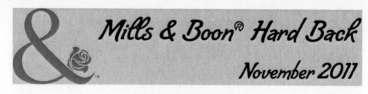

# ROMANCE

| | |
|---|---|
| **The Power of Vasilii** | Penny Jordan |
| **The Real Rio D'Aquila** | Sandra Marton |
| **A Shameful Consequence** | Carol Marinelli |
| **A Dangerous Infatuation** | Chantelle Shaw |
| **Kholodov's Last Mistress** | Kate Hewitt |
| **His Christmas Acquisition** | Cathy Williams |
| **The Argentine's Price** | Maisey Yates |
| **Captive but Forbidden** | Lynn Raye Harris |
| **On the First Night of Christmas...** | Heidi Rice |
| **The Power and the Glory** | Kimberly Lang |
| **How a Cowboy Stole Her Heart** | Donna Alward |
| **Tall, Dark, Texas Ranger** | Patricia Thayer |
| **The Secretary's Secret** | Michelle Douglas |
| **Rodeo Daddy** | Soraya Lane |
| **The Boy is Back in Town** | Nina Harrington |
| **Confessions of a Girl-Next-Door** | Jackie Braun |
| **Mistletoe, Midwife...Miracle Baby** | Anne Fraser |
| **Dynamite Doc or Christmas Dad?** | Marion Lennox |

# HISTORICAL

| | |
|---|---|
| **The Lady Confesses** | Carole Mortimer |
| **The Dangerous Lord Darrington** | Sarah Mallory |
| **The Unconventional Maiden** | June Francis |
| **Her Battle-Scarred Knight** | Meriel Fuller |

# MEDICAL ROMANCE™

| | |
|---|---|
| **The Child Who Rescued Christmas** | Jessica Matthews |
| **Firefighter With A Frozen Heart** | Dianne Drake |
| **How to Save a Marriage in a Million** | Leonie Knight |
| **Swallowbrook's Winter Bride** | Abigail Gordon |

# Mills & Boon® Large Print
## November 2011

# ROMANCE

| | |
|---|---|
| **The Marriage Betrayal** | Lynne Graham |
| **The Ice Prince** | Sandra Marton |
| **Doukakis's Apprentice** | Sarah Morgan |
| **Surrender to the Past** | Carole Mortimer |
| **Her Outback Commander** | Margaret Way |
| **A Kiss to Seal the Deal** | Nikki Logan |
| **Baby on the Ranch** | Susan Meier |
| **Girl in a Vintage Dress** | Nicola Marsh |

# HISTORICAL

| | |
|---|---|
| **Lady Drusilla's Road to Ruin** | Christine Merrill |
| **Glory and the Rake** | Deborah Simmons |
| **To Marry a Matchmaker** | Michelle Styles |
| **The Mercenary's Bride** | Terri Brisbin |

# MEDICAL ROMANCE™

| | |
|---|---|
| **Her Little Secret** | Carol Marinelli |
| **The Doctor's Damsel in Distress** | Janice Lynn |
| **The Taming of Dr Alex Draycott** | Joanna Neil |
| **The Man Behind the Badge** | Sharon Archer |
| **St Piran's: Tiny Miracle Twins** | Maggie Kingsley |
| **Maverick in the ER** | Jessica Matthews |